Just one night, he'd told himself at the time.

To see how it would feel to make love to someone wholesome. Someone who blushed when you looked deep into her eyes. Someone whose attraction for him shocked her enough to make her resign.

Well, he'd found out what it was like—and, come the next morning, he hadn't been able to let her go.

But now the time had come for him to do so.

Time to be cruel to be kind.

"Please don't start sounding like a wife, Amber," he said coldly.

All about the author…
Miranda Lee

MIRANDA LEE was born in Port Macquarie, a popular seaside town on the midnorth coast of New South Wales, Australia, and is the youngest of four children. Her father was a country schoolteacher and brilliant sportsman. Her mother was a talented dressmaker. When Miranda was ten, her father was transferred to Gosford, another coastal town in the countryside, much closer to Sydney.

After leaving her convent school, Miranda briefly studied the cello before moving to Sydney, where she embraced the emerging world of computers. Her career as a programmer ended after she married, had three daughters and bought a small acreage in a semirural community.

Following this, Miranda attempted greyhound training, as well as horse and goat breeding, but was left dissatisfied. She yearned to find a creative career from which she could earn money. When her sister suggested writing romances, it seemed like a good idea. She could do it at home, and it might even be fun!

It took a decade of trial and error before her first romance, *After the Affair,* was accepted and published. At that time, Miranda, her husband and her three daughters had moved back to the central coast, where they could enjoy the sun and the surf lifestyle once again.

Not long into her writing career, Miranda committed herself to writing a six-book series entitled The Hearts of Fire, with a deadline of just nine short months. Bravely, her husband left his executive position to stay home and support Miranda's writing career. He learned to cook and to clean, two invaluable household skills.

Numerous successful stories followed, each embodying Miranda's trademark style: pacy and sexy rhythms; passionate, real-life characters; and enduring, memorable story lines. She has one credo when writing romances—don't bore the reader! Millions of fans worldwide agree she never does.

Miranda Lee

NOT A MARRYING MAN

Harlequin®

TORONTO NEW YORK LONDON
AMSTERDAM PARIS SYDNEY HAMBURG
STOCKHOLM ATHENS TOKYO MILAN MADRID
PRAGUE WARSAW BUDAPEST AUCKLAND

Recycling programs
for this product may
not exist in your area.

ISBN-13: 978-0-373-12989-8

NOT A MARRYING MAN

First North American Publication 2011

Copyright © 2011 by Miranda Lee

This edition published by arrangement with Harlequin Books S.A.

For questions and comments about the quality of this book please contact us at Customer_eCare@Harlequin.ca.

® and TM are trademarks of the publisher. Trademarks indicated with ® are registered in the United States Patent and Trademark Office, the Canadian Trade Marks Office and in other countries.

www.eHarlequin.com

Printed in U.S.A.

NOT A MARRYING MAN

PROLOGUE

Excerpts from Amber Roberts's diary during September of her twenty-fifth year.

Tuesday
What a tiresome day! Arrived at work to find that the hotel had been sold and the new owner would be visiting the premises mid-morning. He's a British businessman called Warwick Kincaid. According to Jill, he's a rather infamous entre-preneur with fingers in lots of pies and a reputa-tion for not holding on to anything for long—his girlfriends as well as his many and varied com-mercial ventures. How she knew all that I have no idea. But then I'm not addicted to gossip mags the way Jill is. Naturally, everyone went into a flap, wondering if their jobs were safe. Not me so much since I'm not all that wrapped in mine. Though I don't want to lose it just at the moment. Hard to save up a deposit on a house without a salary. Anyway, Warwick Kincaid never showed up in the end. Too busy, we were eventually told. Not sure if that's good news or bad news. He's supposed to reschedule for tomorrow.

Wednesday

Well, he showed up this time. Seriously wish he hadn't. What can I say? He's as up himself as I imagined. But younger. Late thirties, maybe forty. He's also the best-looking man I've ever met. I couldn't stop staring at him. He noticed of course. And he stared right back. I've never blushed so much in all my life. He didn't stay all that long but he's coming back tomorrow to talk to all the staff, one at a time, on a mission to find out why a stylish boutique hotel situated in one of the best areas of Sydney isn't turning over a profit. His words, not mine. Jill said afterwards that he fancied me and that I should watch myself. I laughed and told her not to be so silly, that I was in love with Cory and no man, no matter how tall, dark and handsome—or rich—would get to even first base with me. But you know what? When Cory picked me up tonight, I looked at him and didn't feel anything like the buzz I felt today when I looked at Warwick Kincaid. Later, I was relieved when Cory said he wanted an early night. It sounds crazy, but meeting Warwick Kincaid has made me wonder if I'm really in love with Cory. Maybe I'm just in love with the idea of getting married and having the house and family of my own that I've always wanted. It's a worry all right. So's the way I've been fussing over what I'll wear tomorrow. I have a feeling I'm not going to sleep too well tonight. But I have to if I want to look beautiful in the morning. Oh, goodness, did I just think that? Maybe it would be better if I didn't sleep. Must go now. Have to do my nails and put a treatment in my hair.

Thursday

I'm almost afraid to write down what happened today. Because if I do, it will become more real, more powerful, and even more disturbing. Not that anything really happened. I mean, he didn't make a pass at me or anything like that. He just talked to me about the hotel, the same way he talked to everyone else. Seemed happy with my suggestion that the hotel needed some more in-house facilities like a gym and a restaurant. At least a lounge bar where guests could relax and have a drink. On the surface our conversation was strictly business, but all the while those piercing blue eyes of his never left mine. Not for a second. And it wasn't just the way he stared at me. There was something else. I know it wasn't just me. It wasn't my imagination. Something was there, zapping back and forth across the desk that separated us. An electric charge that was both exciting and enervating. When our discussion was over and I had to stand up, I found that my legs had almost gone to jelly. Somehow I made it out of the office and back to the front desk where I slumped down into my chair. I felt faint. I still feel faint thinking about it. And all I've done this evening is think about it. My whole world has been tilted on its axis. How can I get engaged to Cory now when I know that I don't love him? I mean, how could I love him but want to sleep with another man? And I do. I want to have sex with Warwick Kincaid. I can't believe I just admitted that, but what's the point of keeping a diary if you lie to it? So, yes, I want to sleep with Warwick Kincaid. But that isn't love, is it? That's just lust. Can you be in love with one man and in lust with another? Maybe you can. What do I know? I've never felt anything like this before. What I need is to talk to someone about it. Not with my girlfriends, though. They're all silly as wet hens when it comes to the opposite sex. Not Mum, either. She'd be dead shocked. She thinks I'm a good girl. Which I thought I was too, till today. Maybe Aunt Kate. She's seen a lot of life. I'll ring Aunt Kate tomorrow and ask her. She'll tell me how it is, warts and all. Yes, that's what I'll do.

Friday

Well, Warwick Kincaid came back again first thing this morning and totally ignored me, which I found to my disgust upset me terribly. I should have been grateful. Anyway, I was so annoyed with myself that by lunchtime I made the decision to resign. I knew I couldn't work for that man a minute longer. I waited till he was heading for home at the end of the day before I handed him the letter of resignation that I'd typed up during my lunch hour. He read it straight away, then gave me the longest, most intense look. Of course I blushed again. Then he said fine, he accepted my resignation, after which he shocked me rigid by asking me out to dinner tonight. I know I should have said no. I know he's the kind of man who wants pretty young girls like me for one thing, and one thing only. But I didn't say no. I said yes. Because the shocking truth is that I want him for the same thing. I'm not in love with him. Heavens, I'm not sure I even like him. But I'm going to end up in bed with him tonight. I'd be a fool to think he's going to feed me then bring me straight home. On top of that, I have an awful feeling that going to bed with Warwick Kincaid is going to change my life in ways that I can't as yet imagine. There's no point in ringing Aunt Kate now. She can't help me. No one can. I feel like crying. This is not what I want but I can't seem to help myself. Mum thinks I'm going out with Cory tonight so she won't be worried if I don't come home. I always stay at Cory's place on a Friday night. At least I did the right thing by ringing Cory and breaking up with him. I told him that I'd met someone else and that I was sorry. He took the news rather well, I thought, which was of some comfort. But there's no going back now. I've made my bed, so speak, and I'll just have to lie in it…

CHAPTER ONE

July, ten months later...

AMBER'S teeth clenched hard in her jaw as she checked her phone for messages again. Still nothing from Warwick. She punched in his mobile number and was told for the umpteenth time that his phone was not available. She didn't leave a message. There was no point. She'd already left three, each one sounding more frustrated than the last.

When she'd suggested a romantic dinner for two tonight rather than a restaurant meal, Warwick had promised to be home by seven-thirty. But then he'd messaged her shortly before six saying he'd been delayed and that he might be back a bit late, maybe by eight o'clock.

It was now almost nine and still there was no sign of him. No more messages, either.

'Surely you have time to call me,' Amber muttered under her breath as she returned to the kitchen, threw her cell phone onto the black granite counter-top, then switched off the oven in which the already overdone beef stroganoff had been keeping warm.

At least she hadn't started cooking the rice. Maybe the meal was still salvageable. Though her own appetite had long gone.

Opening the oversized stainless-steel fridge, which never held all that much food—not much point when they rarely ate at home—Amber reached for the bottle of New Zealand Sauvignon Blanc, which had become her favourite, and poured herself a glass. Carrying it with her and sipping at the same time, she made her way back through the dining room, grimacing as she passed the beautifully set table before heading for the balcony and the hopefully soothing effect of the water view.

Using her free hand, she slid open one of the glass doors that led out onto the huge curving balcony and that fronted the entire apartment, providing a spectacular view of Sydney Harbour. Unfortunately, it was freezing out there, the stiff breeze that came off the water quickly making a mess of Amber's long hair. Grimacing, she turned and hurried back into the temperature-controlled interior, shutting the glass door behind her. She'd forgotten for a moment that it was winter, Warwick always keeping the apartment pleasantly warm.

Putting her wine glass down on one of the glass-topped side tables that flanked the white leather sofa, Amber made her way across the plushly furnished living room and into the vast expanse of the master bedroom. Her chest tightened as she took in the turned-down bed, the cream satin sheets and the scented candles she'd placed on the bedside tables, in anticipation of the evening ahead.

'Bastard,' she muttered, and marched on into the cream marble en suite bathroom where she took a brush out of the drawer on her side of the twin vanities and began attacking her ruffled hair with angry strokes.

It didn't take her long to put order into her hair which

was easily managed, being long and straight with a blunt-cut fringe.

Her ruffled emotions, however, were not so easily controlled.

Amber could still remember the first time she'd stood on this very spot, looking into this mirror, her blue eyes wide with excitement. It had been the night she'd gone to dinner with Warwick, the night her life had changed for ever...

He'd taken her to a five-star restaurant first, where he'd impressed her with the very best of food and wine, along with his highly entertaining conversation. It'd been impossible for a twenty-five-year-old girl who'd only left Australia for family holidays in Bali and Fiji not to be impressed with this man who'd been everywhere and done everything. Impossible not to be flattered by the fact that someone of his intelligence and status would choose to be with her: Amber Roberts, receptionist.

Afterwards, he'd brought her back here, without bothering to make any excuses, his intentions perfectly clear to Amber as they had been from the moment he'd asked her out.

She'd tried not to appear too blown away, either by his Italian sports car, or his multimillion-dollar Point Piper apartment, which he'd bought two weeks earlier, fully furnished. But she was an ordinary working-class girl who'd been brought up in the western suburbs of Sydney. She wasn't used to this kind of luxury living. She certainly wasn't used to this kind of man.

He hadn't just swept her off her feet and into his bed that night. He'd taken possession of her with a power and a passion that had left her, not only reeling, but ready to say yes to anything he wanted.

But what he'd wanted had been slightly surprising.

She'd feared, when she'd woken in his king-sized bed the following morning, that that might be that. She was sure it would be a case of *hasta la vista, baby*.

Instead, he'd pulled her to him, told her he was crazy about her and asked her to become his girlfriend. Not just in a casual relationship, either. He wanted her to move in with him, travel with him, *be* with him all the time. She wouldn't be able to work, of course. She had to be ready to accompany him at a moment's notice. He travelled quite a lot, both for business and pleasure.

She'd been about to blindly say yes when he'd qualified the terms of the relationship he was proposing.

'Just so you don't get the wrong idea,' he'd added. 'I don't do marriage and children. And I don't do for ever. I have a notoriously low boredom threshold. Twelve months is usually my limit when it comes to any woman. Though with you, my sweet lovely Amber, I just might make an exception. To be honest, you're already one big exception. Up till now, I've never asked a woman to live with me. I dare say it's going to cost me dearly in the end, but there's something about you which I find totally irresistible. So what do you say, beautiful? Do you want to get aboard the Kincaid roller-coaster ride, or not?'

She should still have said no, despite the seductive flattery he'd included in what was really a totally appalling and extremely selfish proposition. But how did a girl say no to more of what she'd experienced the night before? Amber had never known such excitement, or such pleasure. There were things Warwick knew about lovemaking that had quite blown her away. He'd been able to turn her on and keep her that way for hours, reducing her to total mush.

So of course she'd said yes, and now here she was ten

months later, still his live-in girlfriend. Or his mistress, as Aunt Kate had once caustically called her.

But for how much longer?

This was the third time lately, Amber conceded as she stared blankly into the vanity mirror, that Warwick had let her down. A couple of weeks ago, he'd cancelled a weekend getaway to the Hunter Valley that she'd been looking forward to, instead jetting off by himself to New Zealand with two of his business associates to go heli-skiing, a high-risk, thrill-seeking, extremely dangerous sport that had recently cost other lives and that had left her worried sick all weekend. But his worst transgression, in her opinion, had been when he'd refused to accompany her to Aunt Kate's funeral last week, claiming he'd had important business to attend to that day, then adding insult to injury by saying that the old duck hadn't liked him and he hadn't liked her, either!

Which was totally beside the point. Amber had been very fond of her aunt Kate and terribly upset by her aunt's rather sudden death of a stroke. She'd only been seventy-two, hardly ancient.

It had been horrible, sitting in that church all by herself, then having to defend Warwick's absence afterwards. Her relationship with him had already alienated her from her family to a degree. He'd only accompanied her to two family gatherings during the time they'd been together, Christmas Day at her parents' house in Carlingford, and then last Easter, to a family barbecue at her aunt Kate's place up at Wamberal Beach on the Central Coast.

And whilst he'd been quite polite to everyone, he'd somehow made it obvious—to her at least—that he'd been bored rigid. On both occasions they'd been the first to leave.

Amber's two older brothers hadn't pulled any punches last week when it had come to making forthright remarks about her wealthy lover not bothering to attend Aunt Kate's funeral. Even Warwick's lending to her of his flashy red Ferrari for the drive up to Wamberal hadn't softened their disapproval over his absence.

And they'd been quite right. He should have gone with her. His claiming that he'd had important business to attend to that day had just been an excuse. If he'd cared about her at all, he would have made other arrangements and driven her to the funeral himself.

By the time Amber had arrived back home after the wake, she hadn't been able to contain her emotions, telling Warwick exactly what she thought of his lack of sensitivity and support, before flouncing off to sleep in one of the two guest bedrooms.

She'd been half expecting him to come to the room and persuade her back into the master bedroom. But he hadn't. In fact he hadn't made love to her since, which was unusual. When Warwick wanted sex, he could be quite ruthless.

Clearly, he hadn't wanted sex this past week. But she'd wanted him to want it. Wanted him to want *her*.

If she'd been a bolder type of girl, she would have attempted a seduction of her own. But playing the femme fatale was not Amber's style. Although not exactly shy, she never made the first move—although she'd never needed to where Warwick was concerned: he had more than enough moves for both of them.

By now, an increasingly desperate Amber knew she would have to do something to allay her growing fears that he was definitely growing bored with her. Her suggestion this morning over breakfast of a candlelit dinner at home seemed to have gone down well, with Warwick giving her a long lingering kiss at the door before going off to attend to his latest property development.

Not a hotel this time. Warwick wasn't interested in buying another Sydney hotel, despite his earlier acquisition now making a nice profit after he'd put in a gym and a lounge bar, as she'd suggested. This time he'd chosen a night club up at the Cross, a rather run-down, seedy establishment that had definitely seen better days. But Warwick had seen potential in its position and was currently making the place over into the kind of high-class club that would attract the rich and famous with its luxurious ambience, wonderful food and top entertainment. He'd consulted Amber quite a lot about the refurbishing, complimenting her often over her various suggestions. In truth, she was as excited by the project as he was and often accompanied him to the site.

Not this past week, however. He hadn't offered to take her and she hadn't asked. Even if he'd asked her today, she probably would have said no. She'd had other plans.

Amber had known it would take many hours to prepare for the evening ahead. She'd gone to the hairdresser first, after which she'd bought herself a new dress, something extra pretty and feminine. Then she'd had to shop for food, set the table, prepare the bedroom, and, finally, herself.

Oh, yes, Amber thought ruefully as her eyes cleared to rake over her reflection. She'd spent hours on herself, making sure that she looked exactly as Warwick liked her to look.

On the surface, her appearance hadn't changed much since the first day they'd met. Her hairstyle was exactly the same, though she'd given in to Warwick's request to have her honey colour lightened to a cool, creamy blonde. And it did look classier somehow. Her eyebrows were more finely plucked these days, and the make-up she now wore was extremely expensive, not from the supermarket ranges that she used to buy. Although she couldn't see all that much difference, despite the time it took to apply everything. Maybe the lipsticks stayed on a little longer and the mascara was definitely waterproof.

Her figure was still basically the same, longer work-outs in the gym ensuring that all the restaurant food she'd devoured over the past ten months hadn't settled on her thighs or her stomach. Slightly taller than average, Amber had been blessed with a naturally slim body, yet enough curves to attract male attention.

Of course, her wardrobe had changed dramatically, Warwick insisting that she allow him to dress her the way a woman of her 'exquisite beauty' should be dressed. He always called her a woman, never a girl. She'd been powerless to resist his compliments—as she'd been powerless to resist him—and now had a walk-in robe full of designer clothes; something for every possible occasion.

Nothing too sexy, though. Warwick said that true sex-iness was what was hidden, not what was displayed.

A shiver trickled down Amber's spine when she thought about what was hidden under the softly femi-nine Orsini original she was wearing.

The long-awaited sound of her cell phone ringing had her throwing her hairbrush down and racing back out into the living room, where she thought she'd left it. But the sound wasn't coming from there. Had she left the handset out on the balcony? She didn't think she had.

And then she remembered.

'The kitchen!'

Amber prayed for it to keep on ringing as she bolted for the kitchen, wishing that the rooms in this place weren't quite so big.

At last she snatched the phone up into her hands, sweeping it up to her ear and saying, 'Thank heavens you didn't hang up,' rather breathlessly at the same time.

'Er…it's Mum, Amber. Not…who you thought it was.'

Amber suppressed a groan of dismay. Thank goodness she had a call waiting facility or she'd go stark raving bonkers, having to talk to her mother when Warwick might be trying to contact her.

'Hi, Mum,' she said much more calmly than she was feeling. 'What's up?'

Her mother rarely rang her these days, their relationship having become strained since the day she'd announced that she'd quit her job, broken off with Cory and moved in with her billionaire boss.

Amber could well understand why her family didn't approve of her actions and she'd finally given up trying to justify what she'd done. Because there *was* no justification. She couldn't even use love as an excuse. There'd been no love back then, just lust. Though she preferred to think of it as passion—the kind of passion that was as powerful as it was impossible to describe, especially to your mother.

It had been quite a few months before Amber realised she'd actually fallen in love with Warwick. Up till then she'd been so blinded by her desire for the man that she'd been unaware of the deepening of her emotional attachment. The illumination of her true feelings had happened with all the suddenness and force of a bolt of lightning. They'd been staying at a resort in far North Queensland one weekend late last summer, when Warwick had decided to go bungee-jumping. She'd refused to participate herself but had gone along to watch, knowing it was better on her nerves to ac- company Warwick on his thrill-seeking activities rather than stay behind and worry. Something had gone wrong with the length of the rope and his head had almost hit the rocks below. Amber had been absolutely horrified, both by his near miss and the realisation of her love.

Up till then, she'd convinced herself—perhaps as a form of self-protection—that she wouldn't be heart- broken when her time with Warwick was up. After all, broken hearts were for people who truly loved each other. She'd told herself repeatedly that going back to the real world would be difficult, but she would survive.

Suddenly, with Warwick's near-death experience, Amber saw what her life would be like without him. The wool was violently pulled from her eyes and she saw with painful clarity that she'd been fooling herself, big time.

She did love him. Not just truly, but madly and very very deeply.

But she certainly didn't say as much to Warwick, who'd made it clear right from the start that love was no more on his agenda than marriage and children. Quietly, however, like any typical female, Amber had begun to harbour the hope that she might be the exception to that rule as well; that one day he'd discover that he'd fallen madly in love with her too and wanted to keep her for ever. But that hope was rapidly fading.

'Something strange has happened regarding Kate's will,' her mother announced, cutting into her thoughts.

'Oh? What? She left everything to Dad, didn't she?'

Who else? Aunt Kate had been a spinster and Amber's father's only sibling.

'She did in her old will. But it seemed she made a new will, witnessed by those two friends of hers. Max and Tara Richmond. You know who I mean, don't you?'

'Yes, of course.' Amber had first met the Richmonds on Christmas day two years ago, when Christmas dinner had been held at Aunt Kate's place.

Max Richmond was the owner of the Royale chain of international hotels, including the Regency Royale in Sydney, but had semi-retired to the Central Coast after his marriage. He and his wife were good friends of her Aunt Kate. They were a very glamorous-looking couple, with two amazingly well-behaved children: a darling little boy named Stevie and a very pretty blonde baby named Jasmine, who just sat in her stroller and smiled at everyone.

Amber recalled thinking on more than one occasion that they seemed the perfect family.

'You may or may not have noticed,' her mother said, 'but the Richmonds weren't at Kate's funeral last week.'

'No, I didn't notice.' She'd been too upset to notice anything much.

'They were overseas at the time of Kate's death and didn't learn about it till they returned home yesterday. Anyway, to cut a long story short, they immediately got in touch with us to let us know that they were in possession of a new will, made just after Easter this year. In it, Kate has left her superannuation policy to your father, but her home and all its contents go to you.'

'What? But that's not right. I don't deserve it!'

'Whether you deserve it or not is not the point,' her mother said archly. 'Kate's bed and breakfast is now legally yours.'

Amber blinked with shock. Her aunt's B & B was

situated a stone's throw from Wamberal Beach, a much-sought-after location during the warmer months of the year. Any seaside town within a couple of hours' drive from Sydney was never lacking for guests, especially during the school holidays. Aunt Kate had made a good living for herself over the years, though she'd wound the business down a lot lately, because of her age. She didn't even have a website, relying on past customers and word of mouth for guests, plus the sign that stood at the entrance to her driveway. Even if it wasn't a going concern as a B & B any more, the house would still be worth close to a million dollars.

'How does Dad feel about this?' Amber asked worriedly. 'Is he upset?'

'He was at first. Not because he wanted the place himself. As you know, we've done very well with our fencing business over the last few years and we're not wanting for money. But we both thought Tom and Tim should have been included in Kate's will. Yet when your father spoke to them, they said they didn't mind at all. They actually seemed very pleased for you. They pointed out that they weren't close to Kate the way you were. They didn't visit her or love her the way you did. Of course, both my boys have very good jobs,' her mother said proudly. 'They don't need a helping hand. Unlike you.'

'What do you mean by that?' Amber snapped, hurt by the pride that her mother always voiced in Tom and Tim. Doreen Roberts was one of those women who doted on her sons and largely ignored her only daughter. Amber's father was just the same. It was no wonder her sole ambition in life had been to leave home and make a family of her own, one where the love was shared around equally.

'We're all worried about you, Amber, living with that heartless man. Kate was especially worried. I have a suspicion she knew she didn't have long to live, and changed her will in your favour to throw you a lifeline, so to speak. At least you'll have a home and a job when that man's finished with you. Which, if he runs true to form, will be any day now.'

'You don't know that,' Amber threw at her mother before she could think better of it.

'That's where you're wrong, dear. I know quite a lot about Warwick Kincaid and none of it's very complimentary. He might be successful in his business dealings, but his personal life is another matter. It's a case of like father, like son.'

'Meaning?'

'His father was a notorious womaniser who hung himself after losing millions at a casino, according to the inquest.'

Amber was truly shocked. Warwick had told her that his father had died unexpectedly at fifty-one, but she'd just assumed it was from a heart attack or a stroke. He'd said nothing about suicide.

'His wife divorced him soon after their only child was born,' her mother rattled on, 'the price of her freedom being that she had to give up custody of her son. At the time, James Kincaid was one of the richest bankers in England with lots of power and influence. It's all there to read on the Internet if you ever want to look it up.'

'I don't have to, Mum. I know all about Warwick's family background.' Which was an exaggeration of the highest order. Warwick was a man who lived in the here and now. He rarely talked about his past life. Neither did he ask her about hers. He'd told her a few brief details just before Christmas last year when she'd enquired about his family. She did know about the divorce and that his mother—from whom Warwick remained estranged—was an actress of sorts. She knew his mother had never remarried, so he didn't have any half-brothers or -sisters. She knew nothing of his father's womanising, or his suicide.

'Then you must know that your boyfriend's a womaniser as well,' her mother swept on waspishly. 'With a mistress left behind in every country he's lived in. It's a different country each year: France, Spain, Italy, Turkey, Egypt, India, China, Vietnam… And now Australia. Next year he'll probably hop over to New Zealand, then on to the Americas. He's an adventurer, Amber. And a gambler, just like his father. Maybe not at cards or roulette, but with his life. He does dangerous things.'

'Yes, I do know that, Mum,' Amber said ruefully. Bungee-jumping and heli-skiing weren't her lover's only thrill-seeking activities. Warwick liked to drive fast cars and boats. He liked everything that smacked of speed and risk. 'Please, can we stop this conversation right now? You're not telling me anything I don't already know.' Okay, so she hadn't known the detailed itinerary of his past love life, but she'd been warned about his womanising reputation right from the start, both by Jill and Warwick himself.

'And still, you stay with him,' her mother said with incredulity in her voice.

'I love him, Mum.'

It was the first time Amber had said the words out loud to anyone other than herself.

'I very much doubt it,' her mother snapped. 'You're just infatuated with his looks and his lifestyle.'

'You're wrong, Mum. I *do* love him,' Amber insisted hotly. 'And I won't leave him. Not unless he asks me to.'

Her mother sighed. 'There's nothing more to be said on that subject, then. So what are you going to do about Kate's place? You can't just leave it empty indefinitely. You'll have to do something with it.'

'Could I rent it out, do you think? I mean…as a holiday house?' She didn't want to sell it. Not straight away.

'I suppose so. But you'll have to find yourself a reliable agent. And soon. Your father went up there last weekend and mowed the lawns and watered the garden but you can't expect him to keep on doing that. The place is your responsibility now.'

Amber's heart jumped when she heard the familiar sound of the front door being opened. Warwick was home at last. Thank heavens! She was beginning to worry that he might have had an accident.

'Mum, I'm sorry, but I have to go now. I'll come over tomorrow and pick up the keys. Will you be home?'

'Yes. But only till twelve. I have a hairdressing appointment at twelve-thirty.'

'I'll be there before then. Bye.'

Amber tossed the phone back down on the granite counter-top and hurried out of the kitchen, her heart thudding behind her ribs in a maddening mixture of excitement and annoyance.

Just the sight of him tipped her emotions more towards excitement. Warwick was still the most handsome man she'd ever seen, with a strongly masculine face, a well-shaped head, sexy blue eyes, and an even sexier mouth. Combine that with a body to die for and an English accent that could cut glass and you had a man who'd give James Bond a run for his money. In fact, he would make an excellent James Bond in Amber's opinion, his suave man-about-town façade hiding a ruthless inner core. He wasn't totally heartless, as her mother had said. But he was extremely formidable.

It took courage to confront Warwick with anything, even his tardiness. Normally, Amber forgave his tendency to be late for things.

But not this time.

'Where on earth have you been?' she demanded to know. 'You knew I was cooking a special dinner for us tonight. Why didn't you call me? I left enough messages on that damned phone of yours!'

CHAPTER TWO

WARWICK closed the front door behind him, slipping the security chain into place before turning his attention back to his understandably upset girlfriend.

How exquisitely beautiful she looked in that glorious pink dress! Beautiful and desirable. Not that it was a sexy garment, by any means. There was no provocative décolletage on display. The neckline was modestly scooped, and the simple flowing style skimmed rather than clung to her curves, the handkerchief hemline reaching down past her knees.

But never before had a girl turned Warwick on the way Amber could—so damned effortlessly. She didn't have to flirt, or do any of the boldly seductive things his previous women had done. She only had to be in the same room and his hormones jumped to attention.

Suddenly, Warwick wasn't sure if he could continue with the plan he'd started putting into action recently, the one where he showed himself to be the ruthless man he actually was. Much easier to give up on that idea—however perversely noble it was—apologise profusely for being late and do what his body was urging him to do: ravish her all night long.

The temptation was powerful. But so—as Warwick kept discovering to his surprise—was his conscience.

For some time now it had troubled him deeply. Thanks to that wretched aunt of Amber's.

Of course, he himself had known right from the start that it had been wrong to take a girl like Amber to his bed. She'd been too young, too sweet and too sensitive.

But he just hadn't been able to resist her. The chemistry between them had been electric, right from the first moment they'd set eyes on each other.

Just one night, he'd told himself at the time. To see how it would feel to make love to someone wholesome. Someone who blushed when you looked deep into her eyes; someone whose attraction for him shocked her enough to make her resign.

Well, he'd found out what it was like and, come the next morning, he hadn't been able to let her go.

But now the time had come for him to do so.

Time to be cruel to be kind.

'Please don't start sounding like a wife, Amber,' he said coldly as he strode into the room, loosening his tie and undoing the top button of his shirt as he headed for the built-in bar in the corner. 'I texted you that I'd be late,' he threw at her after selecting a glass and reaching for the whisky decanter. 'For pity's sake, woman, don't nag.'

'I…I don't think it's nagging to demand politeness,' she returned in a small, almost crushed voice.

He should not have glanced up at her, not then. Not when her soft blue eyes looked so wounded.

Hell on earth, he couldn't do this. Not tonight. That would be just too cruel.

'You're right,' he said more gently. 'Sorry, sweetheart. I'm a bit wound up. Had to sort out a few problems with one of the building contractors. That's who I was with all this time,' he lied. He'd actually been sitting in a bar in town all by himself, nursing a whisky for two long hours till he was rudely late. 'What say I go shower and change into something more comfortable whilst you rustle up dinner?' he suggested. 'It's not spoiled, is it?'

'No.' Immediately, her dulled eyes glowed with happiness, sending a dagger of guilt plunging into his own wretchedly dark heart.

Oh, Warwick, Warwick, he thought almost despairingly. How are you going to get yourself out of this mess? The girl loves you. Can't you see that?

Yes, of course I can see it, came a frustrated voice from within.

It wasn't the first time this realisation had jumped into Warwick's head. That day he'd gone bunjee-jumping, for instance, when the damned rope had gone awry and he hadn't been killed. More was the pity. Amber's feelings had been written all over her face. She'd been trembling with shock and relief when he was brought back up, unharmed.

Unfortunately, being loved the way Amber loved him—with such sweet sincerity—was as powerful as the most addictive drug. Giving up the way she made him feel was going to take a massive act of will, one that Warwick didn't think he was capable of this evening. Knowing she wanted him to make love to her after dinner was weakening his resolve to end their relationship.

Maybe it was time to tell her the truth about himself, to force Amber to face the fact that there was no future with him.

Could he do that? *Should* he?

Unfortunately, revealing his genetic flaw and all its

appalling inevitabilities might not bring about the desired result. If Warwick had learned one thing about Amber's character during the last ten months, it was that she was as compassionate as she was passionate. She would become visibly upset whenever she saw those ads about poor starving children, and could only be soothed when he promised to make regular donations to whatever charity was canvassing for help. Stories about neglected animals inevitably brought similar distress, as did reports on the news about more bombs killing innocent women and children in war-torn countries. Warwick had taken to putting a box of tissues at the ready by the sofa to mop up her tears.

Finding out what awaited her lover in the future might send her running, not in the other direction, but right into his arms.

It was a risk Warwick decided he could not take. He would have to find some other way to end their relationship.

'Is that your glass of wine over there?' He nodded towards the nearly full glass that was sitting on the side table next to the box of tissues.

'Oh, yes, it is. I was having a drink earlier when I was waiting for you to come home.'

Another stab of guilt. Still, he was here now.

'Bet I can guess what it is,' he said. 'A Sauvignon Blanc from the Marlborough region.'

She smiled as she walked over to pick up the glass. 'You know me too well.'

Yes, he thought as he dropped a few cubes of ice in his glass then slurped in some whisky. I do. And you deserve better than me. You deserve a man who'll marry you, give you children and grow old with you.

I can't do any of those things.

Warwick scowled as he lifted the glass to his lips, irritated suddenly by his maudlin thoughts. What good did they do? He'd always been a realist, and the reality of his life was that he couldn't offer Amber any more than he'd originally offered her.

But damn it all, surely the time she'd spent living with him hadn't been totally wasted. She'd travelled a lot and learned a lot. She'd socialised with some of the world's most successful people, been dressed by the world's most fashionable designers, stayed in the world's most luxurious resorts.

Some women would kill for what Amber had experienced during these past ten months.

Unfortunately, Amber wasn't one of those women. Warwick knew she didn't give a fig about any of those things. All she wanted was his love and his ring on her finger.

Not that *she'd* told him so. Not once.

Her aunt Kate had told him, last Easter at a family barbecue at her home that Amber had dragged him along to.

What an old tartar she'd been. But she'd obviously loved her niece and wanted to see her happy.

'You do realise,' Kate had snapped at him when Amber had left them to go to the bathroom, 'that Amber was practically engaged when she met you. To a perfectly nice boy who would have given her the only things she's wanted since she was knee high to a grasshopper: a loving husband and a family of her own. Two things you'll never give her, Warwick Kincaid.'

The old dragon probably could have said a lot more but didn't get the opportunity.

'Shame on you,' she'd hissed under her breath as Amber had walked back towards them.

That had been three months ago. Warwick hadn't told Amber what her aunt had said. Hadn't asked her about the man she'd been on the verge of marrying. He certainly hadn't embraced the undeniable shame the woman's forceful words had momentarily evoked. Instead, he'd gone on wallowing in Amber's warmth and passion, telling himself that he hadn't forced her to choose him over that other fellow. He'd never forced her to do a single thing. She had free will, didn't she? She *wanted* to be with him.

But gradually, the shame had resurfaced. So had his conscience, something that he'd kept buried for a long time. In hindsight, his plan to stop acting like a besotted bridegroom and start showing his true colours had not been well thought out. He hadn't anticipated the hurt that his abrupt change in behaviour would bring her. Hadn't anticipated his own level of self-disgust.

Far better that the break be clean and swift.

When the time came, that was.

Her walking over and bending forward to pick up her glass of wine showed him that that time definitely wasn't tonight, his flesh stirring as he imagined how she would look doing that *without* that dress on.

'Dinner won't be ready for at least fifteen minutes,' she said as she straightened. 'I haven't cooked the rice yet.'

'What are we having?'

'Beef stroganoff.' Her free hand lifted to push her long hair back from where it had fallen over one of her shoulders. 'I wanted something plain for a change.'

Warwick's flesh stiffened as he noted the telling outline of erect nipples under the pink silk. She was as frustrated as he was, by the look of things. Understandable considering there'd been no sex this past week, the longest time he'd abstained from touching her since their first night together. It had been damned difficult. But at the time he'd been on a mission to make her hate him; to make her give him the flick, instead of the other way around.

Now that that idea had been tossed out of the window, Warwick had no weapons against the desires that were, at this very moment, taking dark possession of him. Various erotic scenarios filled his mind, none of which involved waiting till after dinner to satisfy his already clamouring flesh. His hunger had nothing to do with food. It was primal and sexual and urgent.

'I've changed my mind,' he said abruptly.

'About what?'

'About eating.'

She looked confused. 'You don't want any dinner?'

'Not yet.'

'Then what do you want?'

'I want you to take your dress off.'

Amber's eyes flung wide. 'What?'

Warwick appreciated that he'd never ordered her to take her clothes off for him. Not even in the bedroom. Why now? he wondered, even as he banished any qualms and surrendered to the temptation to exercise his sexual power over her.

'You heard me,' he said in a voice that was as hard as his erection.

'But…but people might see me,' she stammered. 'From out on the water.'

'Not up close,' he countered. 'Come now, Amber, you've nothing to be shy about. You have a glorious body. Do you need a little help, is that it?'

CHAPTER THREE

AMBER just stared at him.

What I need, she suddenly felt like screaming, *is a little respect.*

But no words came from her mouth—her rapidly drying mouth.

She stood there, rooted to the spot, as he started walking towards her, bringing his drink with him, lifting it to his lips and sipping it slowly. Their eyes met over the rim of the glass, his shocking her with their coldness. Or was that desire glittering in their ice-blue depths?

She couldn't be sure. He'd run hot and cold ever since he'd come home, leaving her hopelessly bewildered.

Amber told herself to move. To do something, say something.

Anything!

But her tongue was as useless as her legs.

She remained frozen as he moved around behind her, a soft gasp breaking from her lips when he pushed aside her long curtain of hair, draping it over her left shoulder before bending his mouth to her exposed right ear.

But it wasn't his lips that made her shiver. It was the fear of what she was about to allow…and enjoy.

'Don't,' she heard herself whisper just as his tongue tip dipped into the shell of her ear.

'Don't what?' he whispered a few seconds later.

'Don't do this to me…'

'But you want me to,' he murmured, and nibbled at her ear lobe. 'This is what tonight was all about. Not food.'

'No,' she choked out. 'Not…entirely.'

His laugh was low and sexy. 'Yes. Entirely.'

She stiffened when he ran the zipper down past her waist, a shudder following when he stroked the cold glass he was holding down her spine.

'You want this as much as I do,' he said thickly as he pushed the sides of her dress off her shoulders.

It pooled around her feet in a silky pink puddle, leaving her wearing nothing but her pink high heels.

This wasn't the first time she'd left off her underwear. But it was the first time she'd felt ashamed of having done so.

I'm exactly what Aunt Kate said I am, Amber accepted despairingly as she stood there, naked, before her wealthy lover's gaze. Not a proper girlfriend or a much loved partner, but a mistress, a kept woman. Kept for nothing but her master's sexual pleasure.

Her stomach contracted when he moved around to look at her from the front, her feelings of shame at war with those other wickedly powerful emotions he could so easily evoke. Not just desire but need—the need to be caressed, and kissed, and filled.

She closed her eyes, blotting out the way his glittering blue eyes were gobbling her up. Perversely, her not being able to see him only increased her awareness of her own appalling excitement. Every muscle in her body tensed up, waiting for his touch. Yearning for it. *Dying* for it.

His breath on the nape of her neck told her that he'd moved behind her again. He must have put his drink down too, both his hands free to slide up and down her arms, which immediately broke into goose bumps.

'Do you have any idea what *you* do to *me*?' he murmured as he pressed himself against her naked back, his mouth hovering just above her right ear.

'No,' came her shaky reply. She only knew what he did to her, and what he'd done. Reduced to this…this pitiful state where shame and pride were no match for the pleasure of his lovemaking.

Though this wasn't lovemaking tonight. This was just sex—raw, unadulterated sex.

'If I were a prince in the Middle Ages,' he whispered as he took her hands and lifted them high above her head, 'I would keep you…just like this…locked in a dungeon…with nothing to do but wait for me to come to you.'

She shuddered at the image he'd created.

Why it excited her so much she could not fathom. She should have been repulsed. Instead, she was shaking with excitement.

'Would you like that?' he demanded to know, his breathing growing heavier as he pressed himself even harder against her bare buttocks.

'Yes,' she choked out.

His naked groan betrayed a level of need possibly even greater than her own.

'What on earth am I going to do with you?' he growled.

Amber moaned, having reached that point where pride and shame had become totally irrelevant. She needed Warwick inside her, right then and there, regardless of the fact that she was standing in the middle of a well-lit, glass-walled living room, less than a hundred metres away from where boats full of tourists were enjoying evening dinner cruises on Sydney Harbour.

'Please,' she heard herself practically beg as she moved her legs wantonly apart.

Warwick heard the wild desperation in her voice, felt the uncontrollable excitement that had taken possession of her. He should have felt triumphant. Clever old Warwick, knowing exactly what buttons to press and words to say to seduce her into a state of total surrender.

Why, then, did he suddenly feel bitterly ashamed of himself?

The answer was obvious.

Because she loves you, you bastard. She's not some cheap whore who doesn't care what you do to her.

But even as he told himself all this Warwick was unzipping his trousers. His conscience kept screaming at him not to, but Amber wasn't the only one who'd reached the point of no return.

He groaned as he slid into her, wallowing in the feel of her flesh enclosing his like a tightening fist. She made some sound, a moan perhaps, though not of pain, but of pleasure. It was impossible to stop now. With his right hand splayed firmly over her stomach, and his left cupping her right breast, he began to move his hips.

Not so fast, Warwick, he warned himself as his body immediately surged towards a decidedly premature release. His hips, however, refused to obey him. They jerked back and forth with an urgency that would not be denied, his outspread fingers pressing upwards on her belly, lifting her buttocks up higher against his abdomen, the angle affording him a deeper penetration.

Warwick grimaced as he felt the hot blood rushing along his veins. He was going to come! Hell on earth, he hadn't come this fast in decades!

Amber's suddenly shattering apart in his arms was a huge relief to his pride, allowing him to abandon what little control he had left.

He cried out, holding her tight against him as he ejaculated with the ferocity of an erupting volcano.

She shuddered with him, the contractions of her orgasm more intense, he thought, than ever before. The fantasy he'd painted about keeping her imprisoned in a dungeon had really turned her on. So much so that she'd forgotten who might be watching what they were up to.

You should do this more often, Warwick. Play erotic games with her.

Up till now he'd hardly touched the sides of what he'd learned over many years of hedonistic behaviour. There was so much more he could show her, and do with her.

The only question was…should he?

As much as Warwick was tempted by the thought of becoming Amber's tutor in the erotic arts, he knew that the more imaginative and adventurous practices—whilst wildly exciting—carried a degree of danger; the danger of corruption.

The last thing he wanted to do was corrupt Amber. Pleasure her…yes. Satisfy her…yes. Corrupt her? No.

He would not destroy her basic innocence, he decided as he gently withdrew, then scooped her up into his arms. Such innocence was too precious. *She* was too precious.

He was going to miss her terribly, he thought as he carried her into the bedroom. But not tonight. For now she was still his.

He wouldn't think about the future. Tonight was for nothing but pleasure.

Hers.

His.

But mostly hers.

CHAPTER FOUR

WHEN Amber woke the next morning, all her fears that her relationship with Warwick was coming to an end in the near future had been firmly pushed aside. She smiled as she glanced over at his naked body spreadeagled across the satin sheets, his arms and legs flung wide, his chest rising and falling in the slow, deep rhythm of the truly spent.

Amber could well understand his exhaustion. He'd been insatiable with her last night, showing her with his tireless lovemaking that he was in no way bored with her. It still amazed Amber how well he knew a woman's body and how to uncover a woman's secret desires. There'd been a time—pre Warwick—when she hadn't been that fussed about sex. But, from the first night she'd spent with Warwick, she'd become a virtual slave to the cravings he evoked and satisfied, oh, so well. Amber could not imagine living without the pleasure of his lovemaking…could not imagine living without him!

But you might have to one day, whispered the voice of reason as she slipped out of the rumpled bed and headed for the bathroom.

It was a disturbing thought. What *would* she do when and if that happened?

Amber grimaced, clinging to the hope that maybe it wouldn't. Maybe her dream of Warwick falling in love with her and asking her to marry him was still a possibility. There were times, like last night, when she was confident that he had. There *was* love in his lovemaking: a tenderness and consideration that didn't equate with the cold-blooded womaniser that her mother had more or less described him as last night.

'Oh, my goodness!' Amber exclaimed, bolting back to the bedroom and checking the time on the digital bedside clock.

'Twenty to eleven!' she gasped aloud.

She immediately raced over to shake Warwick on the shoulder.

'Warwick! Wake up! Wake up! I need you.'

He lifted one heavy eyelid, giving her a droll if bleary look. 'You have to be joking, Amber,' he drawled in that cultured voice of his. 'I would have thought you'd had enough for at least twenty-four hours.'

'Not for that, silly!' she said. 'I need you to drive me over to Mum's place before midday, then up to Wamberal. To Aunt Kate's place.'

His second eyelid opened much more quickly, his sleepy expression replaced by bewilderment. 'Run that by me again, would you? I mean…I'm absolutely sure that your aunt Kate is no longer in residence. So why are we driving up to her place?'

'She left it to me,' Amber announced rather baldly. 'In her will. A new one which she'd made recently and which has only just come to light. Mum rang me about it last night but I forgot to tell you. No, don't start asking me endless questions right now,' she raced on when he sat up abruptly with his mouth already opening. 'We haven't the time. We have to be out of here in about fifteen minutes flat if we're going to get to Carlingford before midday. I promised to pick up the keys to Aunt Kate's before Mum leaves to go to the hairdresser's.'

Amber took it as testimony to Warwick's caring that he didn't argue, or tell her that he had more important things to do that day. He just got up and got on with what she'd asked. Just after eleven they were zooming through the harbour tunnel, though Amber was still a little tense that they might not make it in time.

'I'll give Mum a ring once we're out of the tunnel,' she said, and fished her mobile out of her handbag. 'Let her know my estimated time of arrival.'

'So tell me,' Warwick asked with a brief glance her way. 'In your aunt's new will—are you the only beneficiary?'

'No. She left her superannuation policy to Dad. But her house and contents go to me alone.'

'Hmm. I'll bet your mother's somewhat peeved at you being left your aunt's place, rather than her precious boys.'

Amber's head swung round at this quite intuitive remark.

'Did you think I didn't notice the way she favoured your brothers over you?' he swept on before she could say a single word. 'Your father, too. I didn't have to be in their home for more than five minutes to see the lie of the land. Why do you think I couldn't wait to get you out of there on Christmas Day? I'm not good at keeping my mouth shut when I'm bearing witness to such an injustice, especially against someone I care about.'

Amber didn't know what to say. This was the closest

Warwick had ever come to saying that he loved her. She was so touched, a huge lump formed in her throat.

'I...I didn't realise you noticed,' she mumbled at last.

'I noticed all right. The only reason I didn't say something was because it was Christmas, plus I didn't want to give your parents more reason to put you down. They'd already made it patently obvious that they didn't approve of your relationship with me. Not that they said so to my face. I would have thought more of them if they had. Your aunt Kate was a bit of dragon, but at least she loved you enough to give me a piece of her mind.'

'She did?'

'Indeed she did,' he said drily.

Kate had had a reputation for speaking her mind. And a reputation for being a bit of a man hater. Though she hadn't hated all men. She'd liked Max Richmond and had always sung his praises. But then it *was* highly unusual, Amber supposed, for a billionaire to give up his jet-setting lifestyle to get married and raise a family away from the spotlight of wealth and fame.

'What did she say?' Amber asked, though she feared she already knew the answer.

Warwick shrugged his shoulders. 'The usual. I was a selfish you-know-what who should be hung, drawn and quartered for taking a sweet young thing like you as my mistress.'

'Oh,' Amber choked out.

Warwick's head snapped round. 'You're not crying, are you?'

'No,' she denied, but shakily.

'You are,' he said with a sigh. 'I can't stand it when you cry.'

'I don't cry all that often,' Amber said defensively.

'You have to be kidding, sweetheart. You cry at the news, and at ads, and during all those soppy movies you like to watch. I put a box of tissues by the sofa to mop up your tears.'

'They're not real tears. I'm talking about real tears.' She'd only wept a few times since moving in with Warwick. Once, when her mother was highly critical of her relationship. And then, when she'd heard that her aunt Kate had died. Oh, and yes, after her argument with Warwick last week.

But he hadn't been witness to that, had he? He hadn't even been in the same room.

'Tears don't solve anything, you know,' he growled.

'They're not meant to solve anything,' she shot back, dabbing the moisture from her eyes. 'They just happen.'

'I don't like the way women use tears to get what they want.'

'*I* don't.'

'No,' he said, if a little reluctantly. 'You don't.'

'Let's not argue, Warwick,' she said, worried that the happiness she'd felt this morning was beginning to disintegrate.

'Only if you promise not to cry.'

She smiled over at him. 'See? I've already stopped.'

'What about later when you get to your aunt's place?'

'I'll do my best not to.' But she rather suspected she would shed a few tears then. She hadn't been there since her aunt died, the wake having been held at a local club.

'Mmm. I think I should have given you the car for the day. Let you drive yourself up to Wamberal.'

'But I want you with me. I need your advice on what I

should do with Aunt Kate's place. Besides, I don't much like driving your car.'

'What? You don't like driving a Ferrari? Are you insane?'

'I don't like speed the way you do. Promise me you won't go fast when we get on the expressway. There's no reason to. We have all the time in the world.'

Warwick almost laughed. All the time in the world was something he certainly did not have. Which meant he didn't want to spend what precious time he did have with her at Wamberal where she was sure to get weepy over her aunt all over again. Next thing he knew, she'd want to keep the damned place. Maybe even go up there on weekends.

She wanted his advice? Warwick already knew what that advice would be. Put the property in the hands of a good real estate agent to sell, then come back to Sydney with him. He'd already decided he couldn't be without her just yet. Last night had shown him that. He hadn't been able to get enough of her. But maybe soon he'd find the strength to end things. Until then, however, he aimed to keep things exactly as they were, with her by his side, and in his bed.

'I'll wait for you in the car,' he said when they finally arrived at her parents' home in Carlingford just before midday. 'Got a few things to attend to.' And he picked up his BlackBerry.

Amber didn't argue with him. Quite frankly, the last thing she wanted was him by her side when her mother answered the door. She climbed out of the car and hurried up the steep front path to the equally steep front steps. Running up them, she reached the front porch and was about to ring the bell when the door was wrenched open and her mother stood there, looking very annoyed.

'I'd almost given up on you coming,' she said sourly.

'But I rang you from the car to say I'd be here.'

'I don't know why you had to leave it to the last minute,' her mother snapped. 'It's not as though you work.'

Amber could think of nothing to say to that. It was true, after all.

'I'm sorry, Mum,' she heard herself apologising the way she'd been doing all her life. 'We had a late night and we...er...slept in. If you'll just give me the keys I'll be on my way.'

Doreen sniffed her distaste as she swung away and picked up two sets of keys from the nearby hall table. 'Here they are,' she said, and handed them over. 'The second set belongs to Kate's car. That's yours too, it seems.'

'Really?' Amber could not help feeling pleased at this news. She'd only ever owned one car, a rust-bucket she'd bought when she'd been eighteen and had taken a second job as a waitress and needed wheels to get to and from work at night. Naturally, her parents had refused to let her use either of their vehicles. Neither had they offered to subsidise the purchase of one for her as they had with the boys.

It had taken all of her savings—frugally put together when she'd started working at a fast-food restaurant at sixteen—to buy the ancient car, which had broken down within weeks of her purchasing it. After that Amber had decided to do without it and had managed by only ever applying for jobs where public transport was available.

She'd occasionally thought about buying herself another car, but had decided that if she couldn't afford a good one, then she'd rather not have one.

Now, she had her aunt Kate's, which was a very good one, if she recalled rightly, a relatively new white hatchback.

'So what does Lover Boy think of your becoming an heiress?' her mother asked in acid tones.

'Don't call him that, Mum. His name is Warwick and he's very happy for me.'

'I doubt that, dear. Men like that enjoy pulling the strings. The last thing he'll want is for you to have independent means.'

'I don't know why you keep saying such dreadful things about him. What's he ever done to you?'

'It's what he's done to you that I object to.'

'And what's he done to me that's so dreadful? Tim lived with his wife before they got married. And Tom was a real tomcat before he met Viv. It seems to me that you have one set of standards for my brothers and a different one for me. But then, you love them a lot more than you love me, don't you?'

Her mother looked shocked. 'That's not true!'

'Oh, yes, it is, Mum. It's always been true. I'm not sure why. I've tried to be a good daughter. But nothing I've ever done has been good enough. Not that I could ever match it with either of the boys. I wasn't brilliant at school, or at sport the way they were.'

All she'd ever had going for her was her looks, which her mother had rarely complimented her on.

Yet she looked very much like her mother. Or as Doreen had been when she was younger.

It came to Amber suddenly that maybe her mother was jealous of her youthful beauty. Although Doreen

Roberts had aged quite gracefully, she could never compete with a girl thirty years younger.

'I'm sorry you feel that way, Amber,' her mother said stiffly. 'But you're wrong. All I want is for you to be happy.'

'Then you have a strange way of showing it,' Amber said sharply. 'You'd better get going to your hairdresser. I wouldn't want to make you late for anything so important. Bye.'

Amber battled to keep the tears at bay as she whirled and hurried back down the steps, clutching the keys in her hand so tightly that they dug painfully into her palm. Warwick was still on his phone when she climbed into the car, talking no doubt to one of his many contacts. He did most of his business on his BlackBerry.

'Sounds good,' he was saying. 'We'll be there by then. Thanks, Jim.'

'We'll be where by when?' Amber asked as Warwick put his phone away.

'Your aunt's place around two. I've organised for one of the area's top real estate agents to meet us there.'

Amber could not help feeling mildly irritated. Which was crazy. She didn't really want to keep the place, did she? That would be a rather silly decision. An emotional one.

'Did I do something wrong?' Warwick asked.

'No,' Amber replied with a sigh.

'I thought you'd want to sell.'

'I do. It's just...'

'Just what?'

'I don't know, Warwick. Honestly.'

'Your mother said something to upset you.'

Amber laughed. 'My mother always says something to upset me.'

'What was it this time? Something about your relationship with me, I presume.'

'Amongst other things. Look, I really don't want to talk right now. Could you just drive, please?'

'Fair enough. I'll put some music on.'

They didn't exchange a word till the Ferrari hit the freeway north, by which time Amber's distress had calmed somewhat and she turned her mind to the problem of her aunt's place.

'I'm not sure Aunt Kate left me her place for me to sell it,' she said. 'I think she might have envisaged my actually living there and running the B & B.'

Warwick shot her a startled glance. 'Why would she think you would do that?'

'Why not? I've worked in the hospitality industry all my life. I could run a B & B, no trouble.'

'I'm sure you could. But it would be a very lonely existence. After all, now that your aunt has passed away, you have no family up here, or friends that I know of.'

'That's not strictly true. I do know the Richmonds. They live in Wamberal.'

'Who are the Richmonds? You've never mentioned them before.'

'They were close friends of Aunt Kate's. In fact they witnessed her new will. Tara and Max Richmond.'

'Good Lord, you don't mean Max Richmond, the hotel magnate!'

'Yes. Do you know him?'

'I know *of* him. I had heard on the grapevine that he'd sold off most of his international hotels and retired somewhere. I just didn't know where. I rather imagined the Riviera or Monte Carlo, not Wamberal Beach. Did he marry a local girl, is that it?'

'No. I'm sure Tara was a Sydney girl. Aunt Kate

told me a little about their romance. Apparently, she and Max had been dating for some time when Tara fell pregnant quite accidentally. But she was afraid Max wouldn't believe her and ran away, to Aunt Kate's B & B. It seems seriously rich men are paranoid about gold-diggers trying to trap them into marriage with a baby. Is that true?' she asked Warwick, such a thought having never occurred to her before. She religiously took her pill every evening, not believing in having children unless you were happily married. Nowadays she always carried a spare packet of pills with her in her handbag in case Warwick swept her off on one of his impulsive overnight getaways without her having a chance to go home and pack properly.

'Perfectly true,' Warwick replied drily.

'I would never do something like that,' she said firmly.

'I know you wouldn't. Obviously, Max Richmond came to the conclusion that his girl wouldn't, either.'

'Oh, yes, I was telling you about them, wasn't I?'

'I presume they got married and lived happily ever after.'

'As far as anyone can tell. They always look the perfect family. They have two children now, a little girl as well as their son.'

'If they were such good friends of your aunt, why weren't they at her place last Easter? I'm sure I would have remembered them if they were.'

'They were overseas. They travel quite a bit. They were actually away when Aunt Kate died.'

'So Richmond hasn't given up the hotel industry entirely?'

'Not quite. He still owns hotels in Asia and the Regency Royale in Sydney. He has a penthouse apartment there which Aunt Kate stayed in once. She said it was gorgeous.'

'How old would Richmond be? Forty?'

'Mid forties, I'd say.'

'And his wife?'

'I'm not sure. Thirty something. And drop-dead gorgeous.'

'Not surprising. Seriously rich men don't marry plain girls.'

Some don't marry at all, Amber almost shot back, just biting her tongue in time.

'I'm not surprised Richmond hasn't totally retired,' Warwick went on. 'He'd be bored if he stayed home every day, twiddling his thumbs. You'd be bored too, Amber, running a B & B. Bored and lonely.'

'But I'd meet people.'

'For one night only. Come the next morning they'd be up and gone. Running a B & B is a job for a couple. Or an old maid like your aunt was. It wouldn't suit you at all. Surely you're not seriously considering doing it.'

'That depends…'

'On what?'

Amber hesitated to answer for a long moment. When she'd woken this morning, she'd been very quick to put aside her worries over Warwick's very selfish behaviour of late. Listening to her mother's low opinion of her lover's character, however, had revived all her doubts about the depth, plus the lasting nature, of their relationship.

The temptation to keep putting her head in the sand was acute. She loved Warwick and didn't want what they had to end, however short-lived that might be. But a little voice in her head kept nagging at her to stop being naïve and so disgustingly weak.

Nausea swirled in her stomach at the prospect of

finding out she was skating on thin ice where he was concerned. But it had to be done sooner or later.

'It depends on how long our relationship lasts,' she said at last.

'I see,' he bit out.

Amber tried to gauge what he meant by that. But it was hardly a forthcoming statement, which was so typical of Warwick.

'I know you don't like talking about the future,' Amber went on, suddenly determined to have things out with him. 'I've done my best to live in the moment the way you do. But I'm not really like that, Warwick. I've always been a practical person, a planner. This past ten months with you have been marvellous and I'll never regret them. But I need to know if I have any chance of a future with you. I gave up everything to live with you: my job, a boyfriend I was going to become engaged to, my friends. Even my family, to a degree. When and if we break up, I'll have nothing.'

CHAPTER FIVE

WARWICK wished later that he'd thought before he'd opened his mouth. But, at the time, it annoyed him that Amber thought he would dump her with nothing.

'If and when we do break up, Amber,' he snapped, 'you will be well looked after. I have every intention of giving you the Point Piper apartment. *And* this car.'

Even if he hadn't glanced over and seen her face go a ghastly shade of grey, the sound of her shocked gasp warned him that his offer of a generous parting settlement did not please her.

Which he should have realised. For goodness' sake, the girl was obviously in love with him. It was perfectly understandable that Amber wouldn't want to be treated like some gold-digging mistress who was only with him for what she could get out of it, when all she actually wanted was love and marriage. And his children, no doubt.

Her aunt Kate had spelled out the truth for him. Why did he keep forgetting?

Once again Warwick was tempted to reveal everything. But the thought of seeing pity in Amber's eyes repulsed him. He'd rather see dislike, or even outright hatred.

'I gather that suggestion doesn't find favour with

you?' he said in a tone of voice that she could only interpret as indifferent.

Amber struggled for composure. She'd thought he could not hurt her any more than he had with his disgustingly materialistic offer. But, suddenly, she felt not just cheap but almost worthless.

'Did you expect that it would?' she threw at him.

He shrugged his shoulders. 'I have learned to expect the unexpected when it comes to women.'

Amber stared over at him. Was this the same man who'd made love to her so tenderly the night before?

Her family had been right. He was heartless. And she... she was a fool!

But no longer. Her own heart hardened towards him as she pushed aside her distress for the moment and considered her options.

Her decision surprised her.

'In that case,' she said boldly, 'you will be delighted to hear that I will quite happily accept your apartment as my fee for services rendered. But I do not want this car,' she swept on. 'I have Aunt Kate's now, if you recall.'

'I doubt it's a Ferrari,' he retorted.

'No. But, quite frankly, I'm not overly fond of Ferraris. If you don't mind, I'd like you to slow down. You're breaking the speed limit. And whilst I don't give a damn if you lose your driving licence, I do not want to lose my life.'

He did ease off on the accelerator a little but the Ferrari still zoomed across the Hawkesbury River bridge doing a hundred and twenty kilometres an hour, ten kilometres over the speed limit.

'On top of that,' she continued, her heart pounding inside her chest, 'once we reach Aunt Kate's place, we're finished! The thought of living with a man like you for another single day makes me feel sick.'

'For heaven's sake, don't be such a drama queen! You knew the score when you moved in with me. Don't pretend you didn't.'

'I won't. But I thought things had changed. I thought you cared about me, the same way I...I care about you.' She bit her trembling bottom lip, determined not to cry, or to blurt out that she loved him.

'I do care about you,' he insisted. 'If I didn't, I wouldn't be prepared to give you a five-million-dollar apartment. Which, I might add, you haven't refused. Not that I would have admired you if you had. I would have thought you a naïve little fool.'

'Which is what I was all this time. But not any more. I've finally had my rose-coloured glasses taken off where you're concerned.'

'Good,' he ground out. 'It's about time.'

She stared over at him. 'You've been planning to break up with me for a while, haven't you?'

He stayed silent for a few seconds, a frown drawing his dark brows together.

'I admit I've become concerned that you were getting emotionally involved with me,' he said at last.

'And that would be dreadful, wouldn't it?' she threw at him.

'Yes,' he said. 'It would.'

'But why?' she demanded to know, frustration and exasperation fuelling her tongue. 'What is it about commitment which terrifies you so much?'

'The fact that I wouldn't be able to sustain it and then I'd feel guilty. It's a case of like father, like son, Amber. My father was, to put it bluntly, a notorious womaniser.'

'That's a cop-out. Just because your father was a no-torious womaniser doesn't mean you have to be one.'

'There is a saying, Amber, "The apple doesn't fall far from the tree." I am the spitting image of my father, in every way. Trust me on this. Look, I never planned to hurt you. But I've realised that I will, if you stay with me much longer. You're a truly nice girl and you deserve someone better than me, someone who will love you and give you what you really want. Which isn't being a rich man's mistress.'

Amber blinked her surprise.

'Are you saying you're being cruel to be kind?'

'I am rarely kind, Amber. But with you, it's hard not to be. So, yes, I probably am being just that.'

Amber's head whirled with a thousand conflicting thoughts. She couldn't work out what it was he felt for her.

'I don't understand you, Warwick,' she said at last.

'Don't even try, sweetheart.'

'Don't call me that,' she snapped. 'I hate it when you call me that.'

'What's wrong with it?'

'It makes me feel cheap.'

'Don't be bloody ridiculous!'

A taut silence fell between them, neither speaking a word till the Ferrari turned off the expressway and made its way down the hill towards Gosford, which was the doorway to the central coast with all its lovely beaches. Not a beach town itself, Gosford surrounded a large expanse of inland water, which on that day was very still and blue.

'It's a pretty place,' Warwick commented as he drove over an arched bridge that had the water on his right and a palm-lined sports stadium on his left.

'What?' Amber's mind was not on her surroundings.

'Gosford. It's a pretty town.'

'I suppose so.'

'Do you want to stop somewhere for lunch?' he asked.

Amber glanced at her wristwatch. It was just after one. But she didn't feel at all hungry. Distress always destroyed her appetite. Given her present circumstances, she doubted she'd ever eat again.

'I'd rather go straight to Aunt Kate's place if you don't mind. Do you remember the way?'

'I follow the coastal road till we get to a roundabout at Wamberal where I turn right, after which I turn left onto the road which runs beside the lake. Your aunt's place is just along there on the right.'

'You have a good memory for someone who's only been there the once.'

'I have a photographic memory.'

The remark surprised Amber. Warwick rarely talked of himself in that way. Although obviously very clever, he wasn't a braggart.

'Did your father have a photographic memory?' she asked, recalling his earlier insistence that he was the spitting image of his father, in every way.

'Actually, no,' came his surprising reply. 'I got that from my mother. She was an actress. Apparently, she only had to read a script through once to remember it word for word. Or so my father told me. I had no reason to doubt him, since I've inherited a similar talent. It made studying for exams a lot easier, I can tell you.'

'I suppose you were brilliant at school,' Amber said, thinking to herself how odd it was that they were talking like this. During the ten months they'd lived together, they'd never had a conversation of this vein. Warwick had always cleverly sidestepped any questions about his family, or his past life.

'Yes,' he admitted. 'I was head boy of my school.'

She wasn't surprised.

'I wasn't very good at school,' Amber said with a sigh. 'That's why I left when I was sixteen.'

'Being good at school is not all it's cracked up to be. I've seen lots of people who were brilliant academically but had no street sense. And very little common sense, either. You are an extremely capable and clever girl who, I'm sure, could turn her hand to anything. And you have social skills which are invaluable. People like you. You're quite right when you said you could run your aunt's B & B. You could do it standing on your head.'

But I don't *want* to run my aunt's B & B, Amber felt like wailing. I want to stay with you. I *love* you.

But there was no point. It was over, all her futile hopes of Warwick falling in love with her dashed to the ground. And whilst she didn't feel as angry with him as she had a little while before, there was no point in pretending that she'd ever meant anything more to him than a very pretty girlfriend who'd provided him with an accommodating social companion, an agreeable hostess when required and lots of sex.

Of course, it had been the lots of sex part that had turned her head and confused her heart. It had been oh-so-easy to imagine that his lust for her might one day turn to love. Hers had for him, after all. But super-rich men like Warwick, Amber realised, were of a different ilk. He wasn't looking for love, or commitment, just entertainment.

It was a depressing reality, made all the worse because in her mind she could hear her parents and her brothers saying, 'I told you so!'

Still, maybe they'd shut up when she gave them a whole heap of money from the sale of the Point Piper apartment. She didn't doubt that Warwick would give her the property. In a perverse way, he did have honour. And honesty. Also, she could not deny he had told her the score right from the beginning. He'd warned her that he didn't do for ever. She'd been stupid to ignore his warnings. Now, she would have to nurse a broken heart for a long time.

That breaking heart squeezed tight at this last thought, bringing home the harsh reality of life without the man she loved. The future ahead looked bleak, and empty, and infinitely depressing.

Maybe it would be a good idea for her to stay up here and run her aunt's B & B. Alternatively, she could put the B & B on the market, then take a flat somewhere in Sydney and look for a job. She had a wide range of experience in the hospitality industry, from waitressing to bar work to fronting reception desks in hotels and clubs. It shouldn't take her too long to find employment. Even if it took a while, she still had the apartment and her savings, which she hadn't touched since meeting Warwick.

But she didn't have the heart—or the courage—to put herself out there like that. Not right now. She really needed to be by herself for a while to grieve the death of all her secret hopes and dreams. What better place than her aunt's home, which would be very peaceful and quiet at this time of the year? She didn't have to try to run the B & B straight away. She could just potter around the house for a month or so. Go for long walks on the beach. Read some of the many wonderful books her aunt had collected over the years.

Maybe she'd even start keeping a diary again…

She'd given that up when she'd moved in with Warwick. Which, she should have realised, was a telling thing to do. Subconsciously, she must have known that her time with him was just a fantasy, and not of the real world.

Amber was glad that she hadn't kept a record of her stupidity. It would have hurt too much to read it over, which she no doubt would have now.

'We don't have to break up just yet,' Warwick said suddenly, startling her out of her musings.

Amber stared over at him. First at his handsome profile. Then at his long strong fingers, which were curled over the steering wheel; those same fingers that last night had given her such pleasure.

The temptation to stay with him for as long as possible was overwhelmingly strong. But how could she without sacrificing what little pride she had left?

It wouldn't be the same anyway, she argued to herself. I'd know I was on borrowed time. I'd end up hating him. And myself. Better a clean break now. Better to say goodbye with some dignity.

'No, Warwick,' she said, her voice surprisingly firm. 'I think it's better that we call it quits today. You can drop me off at Aunt Kate's and go straight back to Sydney.' The sooner he was out of her sight, the better. Not that out of sight would be out of mind.

'Just like that?' he returned, sounding not at all pleased. 'What if I don't want to break up today? And what if I don't want to go straight back to Sydney? You might at least have the decency to offer me a cup of coffee and a trip to the loo. We've been on the road for some time.'

Amber sighed. He was right. Now that she thought about it, she too wanted to go to the bathroom. But he could forget the coffee. She wasn't going to give him a single opportunity to try to change her mind. There were plenty of places along the highway where he could get himself some refreshment. Once he was finished in the bathroom, she would insist that he go.

Suddenly, she realised he'd missed the turn.

'You've just gone through the roundabout!' she exclaimed frustratedly. 'You didn't turn right…'

CHAPTER SIX

WARWICK swore. He hated feeling a fool, and he felt like one at that moment. What in hell was wrong with him, finding all sorts of excuses to prolong things? Far better that he just drop her off and leave. He could easily use the restroom at the garage they'd just passed. Nothing would be gained by accompanying Amber into Aunt Kate's property.

Nothing admirable, anyway, he realised, his thoughts turning dark.

Damn it all but he wanted her. Maybe more since she'd declared her intention to have done with him. How perverse was that? He should have been relieved that it was over, without any big scenes. He'd been half afraid that when the dreaded moment came Amber would dissolve into tears, or become hysterical and declare that she loved him and couldn't live without him.

Instead, she'd been amazingly strong and decisive. Warwick had been somewhat surprised that she'd agreed to accept the apartment. Though frankly if she'd knocked it back that would have shown her to be a romantic idealist with no common sense at all.

Instead, she'd given him a glimpse of an Amber he'd never encountered before. The girl sitting beside him at this moment—the one who dared to call it quits with *him*—wasn't the sweet, soft, amenable creature he'd been living with this past ten months. This girl was far more formidable. And, he was finding, even more attractive to him.

When he glanced over at her flushed cheeks and defiantly upturned chin he experienced a surge of desire even more intense than he had the night before. The thought that he would never make love to her again was simply not on. So was the idea that he would be leaving her up here and driving back to Sydney alone.

'There's a set of lights coming up,' Amber said. 'Turn right there and I'll direct you to Aunt Kate's the back way. It won't take much longer.'

'No sweat,' he replied. 'I'm not in any hurry.' And he glanced over at her again.

When Amber's head turned and her eyes met his, her heart jolted in her chest. She knew that look, knew what it meant.

Over my dead body, she thought angrily, even as that same body instinctively responded, as Warwick had programmed it to this past year. Her heartbeat quickened, her belly tightening, as did her nipples.

She could not let him go inside Aunt Kate's with her, she accepted immediately. That would be the kiss goodbye to her resolve to have done with him today. He was way too good at seduction—and she was way too weak once in his arms—for her to risk being alone with him in a house with bedrooms.

Amber steeled herself as she issued brusque directions to her aunt's place.

She should have foreseen that he wouldn't like her being the one to break up with him. It would have piqued his ego. Which was the reason behind that sexually charged look. His massive male ego insisted that *he* had to be the one to do the breaking up in his relationships. *He* made the rules and *he* made all the decisions.

Well not this time, buster, Amber vowed. I might have been a pushover once, but not any more. I've always despised girls who go back to boyfriends who've treated them badly, trotting out the excuse that they love them. If loving someone means you let them treat you without respect, then I don't want any part of that kind of love.

Not that she deserved his respect, came the sudden shaming realisation. In his eyes she was obviously no better than all his previous—mistresses. Worse, really. Hadn't she moved in with him without a single promise of anything but fun and games? He'd warned her right from the start that their relationship was temporary. Yet she'd still agreed. And now…now here she was, prepared to accept payment for services rendered.

How cheap could you get?

Not that her own behaviour exonerated Warwick's. His admitting that he was a callous womaniser didn't make it right.

Still, as long as silly girls like herself allowed him to use them shamelessly, then pay them off, he would continue going from woman to woman as powerful men had been doing since time began.

'I know the way from here,' Warwick said when they turned into Ocean View Drive.

Thirty seconds later they were driving down her aunt's street, which ran alongside the lagoon.

The sight of the sign announcing Kate's B & B brought a lump to Amber's throat. How strange it would be not to have Aunt Kate open the door with her wonderfully welcoming smile.

Warwick turned the Ferrari into the driveway, which led into the large back yard where there was plenty of room for guests and visitors to park. Because of the way the house was located on the block, the back door had always been used as the front door. Warwick drove right up close to the back porch whilst Amber glanced around the yard.

Despite her father having mown the lawn recently, some of the flowerbeds were looking unloved. Aunt Kate had been an avid gardener and would never normally have let her roses go unpruned during the winter months. She must have felt unwell for quite some time to neglect her garden this way.

Sadness overwhelmed Amber as she looked up at the back of the two-storeyed house with its drawn curtains and general air of emptiness. A sigh—almost a sob—escaped her lips.

'I knew it,' Warwick said rather impatiently after he cut the engine. 'You're going to cry.'

It infuriated her, his lack of compassion where her aunt's death was concerned.

Her head whipped round, her blue eyes now blazing with fury.

'Not in front of you, I won't be,' she snapped, snatching her handbag up from the floor and opening the passenger door. 'Don't bother getting out,' she swept on, when his hand went towards the handle on the driver's door. 'You're not coming inside. I don't want to see you ever again.'

His eyes narrowed as he glared over at her. 'Is that so? What about the apartment? I'll have to see you again, if you want that.'

'Actually, I've been thinking about your most generous offer,' she lied on a surge of anger. 'I've decided I don't want it. I don't want anything from you, Warwick Kincaid, except your absence from my life.'

'You don't really mean that. You're just angry with me at the moment.'

'Too right I am.'

'You don't have any right to be. I haven't treated you badly.'

'You used me and you know it.'

'I told you what kind of man I was up front. I warned you that I didn't do love and marriage, or for ever. You seemed happy enough to still come along for the ride.'

Amber shook her head in a kind of despair. 'Yes, I did. And I feel deeply ashamed of myself for doing so. All I can say in my defence is that I didn't really believe you could be that cold-blooded.'

'I'm not cold-blooded, as you very well know.' And he gave her that desire-filled look again.

Amber clenched her jaw hard. 'I don't want to have this conversation any more, Warwick,' she ground out. 'It's over. We're over. Just go.'

'I don't want to leave you like this,' he said, scowling.

'I'll well aware of that! I know what you want, Warwick Kincaid. But you're not getting it. Ever again.' She climbed out of the car and slammed the door. 'If you don't go, I'll call the police.' And she fished her mobile out of her bag.

'I'll ring you,' he said.

'Please don't.'

'You can't stop me ringing you.'

'I'll buy a new phone.'

'How will you afford that?'

'I have money, Warwick,' she enjoyed telling him. 'You think my life began the moment you walked into it? I have almost twenty thousand dollars in my savings account. I'll survive very well without your wretched apartment!'

'What about your clothes? And your jewellery?'

'I don't want them, either. Maybe you can recycle some of it for your next mistress.'

He glowered up at her before starting the engine. 'This isn't the end of us, Amber Roberts,' he threatened in an ominously low voice. 'I'll be back once you've calmed down.'

Amber gripped her handbag defensively in front of her as she watched him do a rather savage U-turn, chewing up some of the grass as he accelerated out onto the road and sped off.

For almost a minute, she just stood there, listening to the slowly decreasing noise of his angry departure, till finally the only sound she heard was the low hum of distant traffic.

It was then that she started to cry, deep wrenching sobs, which she feared the neighbours might hear. There were houses on either side.

Not wanting contact with anyone at that moment, Amber dropped her phone back into her bag and snatched up the keys to the house. Naturally, the key to the back door was the last one she tried. By the time she locked the door behind her, her weeping had subsided somewhat.

But not her distress. Amber dropped her handbag onto the hall table before burying her face in her hands.

'Oh, Warwick...Warwick,' she cried heartbrokenly.

He had vowed to come back. But she doubted that he would. That had just been his ego talking again. Once he thought about it more rationally, he'd see that there was no point in trying to keep their relationship going. Not when it was obviously on borrowed time. As soon as Warwick realised he'd disposed of his Australian mistress very cheaply indeed, he would be a fool not to cut and run.

And Warwick was no man's fool.

Despite knowing that their break-up was all for the best, such thinking depressed Amber. She'd honestly believed that he'd come to care for her; that she meant more to him than just a temporary plaything, to be bought off when he tired of her, or when she committed the unforgivable sin of becoming 'emotionally involved'.

Amber noted, however, that even then Warwick couldn't bring himself to say the world *love*. It was some comfort to her own pride that she'd never told him she'd fallen in love with him. Now, she never would.

She sighed as she lifted her head from her hands.

'Maybe I should have accepted the apartment,' she muttered dispiritedly. 'People will think *me* a fool for ending up with nothing.'

But if she had taken it, then she would have become what everyone had probably been calling her behind her back. A rich man's whore. At least she did have her pride, which, she supposed, was something.

Or was it?

What was that saying about pride being a lonely bedfellow?

Her mobile phone suddenly ringing was a telling moment. For in that split second Amber became brutally aware that pride was not as powerful as love. The truth was she *wanted* it to be Warwick calling her. She wanted him to come back.

Unable to stop herself, she hurriedly retrieved her phone from her handbag and flipped it open, her heart thudding loudly behind her ribcage.

'Yes?' she choked out.

'It's me, Amber. Your mother.'

'Oh…' Impossible to keep the disappointment from her voice, or the dismay from her heart.

'Are you at Aunt Kate's yet?' her mother asked abruptly.

Amber sighed. 'Yes.'

'Look, I forgot to tell you that Max Richmond wants you to give him a call. Kate used his solicitor, it seems, to make her new will and there are papers you will need to sign to transfer the house and car, et cetera, into your name.'

'Fine,' she said wearily. 'Do you have his number?'

Amber put the number into her menu.

'Is that all, Mum?'

'Yes. No. I…er…can you talk for a moment?'

'What about?'

'Well…I've been thinking about the things you said to me today and I feel really terrible. I do love you, Amber. Yet I can see why you might think I favour the boys. Please…I'd like to try to explain how it was when you came along.'

Did her mother honestly think she didn't know how it had been? She was well aware that her father had wanted to stop having children after the two boys were born. He'd only ever wanted sons, according to a conversation she'd once overheard. She'd been an accident, then had compounded things by turning out to be a girl, an unsporty, non-academic girl who just couldn't compete with her overachieving, highly competitive brothers.

'Mum…please…I don't want to have this conversation right now.'

'You know, Amber,' her mother said, back to her usual stroppy tone. 'Ever since you got mixed up with that man, you never have time to talk to me.'

Amber momentarily considered telling her mother that she'd broken up with Warwick, but fortunately stopped herself in time. No way could she stand the third degree over what happened. Or all the inevitable recriminations.

'We've only just arrived, Mum, and I haven't even had time to go to the toilet. I'll give you a call later.'

'Promise?'

'Yes,' Amber said, her chin beginning to wobble dangerously. 'Bye for now.' She choked back a strangled sob and hung up, after which she turned her mobile off.

For a long time she just stood there, clutching the phone and staring into space. The tears didn't come, thank heaven. But she felt awful over the way she'd reacted to the phone ringing. How could she possibly want Warwick back? He was a bastard. An arrogant, selfish bastard!

And yet she'd fallen in love with him. Why? What had he ever done to deserve her love?

Okay, so he was a good lover. No, a *great* lover, she had to admit.

Amber shook her head from side to side. Was her so-called love for Warwick based on nothing more substantial than sexual pleasure? If so, then she was a terribly shallow person.

Her mind searched for other qualities Warwick possessed that deserved loving.

He was honest. She had to give him that. He'd never lied to her. At least, she didn't think he had. He was also very generous, dispensing great chunks of money to this and that charity every other week.

But then, he could afford to, couldn't he? came a cynical voice in her head. Easy to be generous when you were filthy rich.

What kind of man would he have been if he'd been born poor?

Amber decided it would be an interesting experiment to somehow put Warwick in a position where his life wasn't so damned cushy. How would he handle adversity? Would it bring out the worst, or the best in him?

Amber shrugged her shoulders. She would never find out, would she? He was gone. Gone from her life, though not from her heart. She *did* love him, unfortunately. Love, it seemed, wasn't always subject to reason, or reasons. It just was.

At last she dropped her phone back into her bag and made her way slowly along the hall to the tiny downstairs toilet, which was tucked under the staircase.

As she washed her hands afterwards the small mirror above the equally small hand basin showed nothing of the sadness she was feeling. She actually looked good, her bout of tears not having lasted long enough to bring on puffiness or dark circles. Finger-combing her windblown hair into place, she made her way back along the hall into her aunt's roomy country-style kitchen to make herself a cuppa. There she took off her leather jacket and draped it over the back of a wooden kitchen chair before filling the kettle with water. She was just getting a mug down from the pine cupboard above the counter when the doorbell on the back door rang.

Once again, that shocking vulnerability hit home. She practically ran to the door, despising herself even as she flicked open the lock and wrenched the door wide.

It wasn't Warwick. The tall, good-looking man standing on the back porch was a perfect stranger.

CHAPTER SEVEN

'YES?' Amber said, unable to keep the dismay from her voice.

'Hi there,' he said, and flashed his business card. 'I'm Jim Hansen, from Seachange Properties. I have an appointment to meet Mr Warwick Kincaid here at two p.m.'

Amber suppressed a groan. She'd forgotten about Warwick's organising this meeting.

'Hello,' she said, using the practised smile that she'd perfected during her various jobs in the hospitality industry where you smiled no matter how lousy you felt. 'I'm Amber Roberts, the new owner here, actually, not Mr Kincaid. I inherited it from my aunt who died recently.'

'Ah. I didn't realise. Sorry,' he said.

'I dare say Warwick didn't enlighten you.'

'No, he didn't,' the agent returned. 'I thought he was the owner. So will your boyfriend be handling the sale for you, Ms Roberts?' he asked.

'Absolutely not,' she returned somewhat brusquely. 'And Warwick's not my boyfriend. He's just a friend who drove me up here today. He's already gone back to Sydney.'

The agent smiled the kind of smile men often smiled

at Amber. 'In that case this is for you, Ms Roberts,' he said, handing her the business card. 'Or can I call you Amber?'

'Amber will be fine.'

'Great. I gathered from my conversation with Mr Kincaid that you want to sell—is that right?'

'Well, to be honest, Mr Hansen—'

'Jim,' he interrupted smoothly.

'All right. *Jim*,' she said, irritated slightly at the agent's confidence. She was rather tired of confident men. 'To be honest,' she went on, 'I'm not sure yet what I'm going to do with my aunt's place. I only found out last night that I'd inherited it. I'm afraid Warwick just presumed I would want to sell straight away and took it upon himself to contact you without my say-so. I'm sorry that you've wasted your time coming out here today.'

'There's absolutely no need for you to rush such an important decision,' Jim said affably. 'But since I'm already here, why don't you give me a quick tour around the place? That way, I could give you an up-to-date valuation. Then you'll know what to expect, if and when you do decide to sell.'

Amber almost said no, which was crazy. It was a sensible move to get a valuation. On top of that, if she sent him away she would be alone again. Alone and sad. Better to do something constructive and distracting.

'That sounds like a good idea,' she said. 'Look, I was just about to have a cup of coffee. Care to join me?'

'Love to.'

'This way,' Amber said and led him into the kitchen.

'Nice-sized room,' the agent said as he pulled out a kitchen chair and sat down.

Ten minutes later, Amber was almost regretting

asking the man to stay. He wasn't exactly chatting her up. But he was exhibiting the kind of super-slick charm that successful salesmen invariably possessed.

Amber was in no mood to be charmed, or flattered.

'If you've finished your coffee, Jim,' she said, standing up abruptly, 'I'll give you that quick tour of the house and you can tell me what you think it's worth.'

'Okay,' he agreed readily, and stood up also.

'Well, as you can see, this is the kitchen,' she started in a businesslike fashion. 'I guess you'd describe it as country-style. Now, if you follow me I'll show you all the downstairs rooms first.'

The downstairs consisted of a dining room and lounge room at the true front of the house, which faced north-east, towards the beach. At the back of the house was the kitchen-cum-breakfast room, across from which was a very large room, which had once been a games room, but which Aunt Kate had had converted several years ago into her own bedroom, complete with sitting area and her own private bathroom.

Upstairs had also been renovated around the same time, Aunt Kate having decided to change her establishment from a modestly priced guest house into a more upmarket B & B. The original five-bedroom, two-bathroom layout had been changed into three large bedrooms, each with its own en suite bathroom, along with a very nice sitting room where one wall was totally devoted to bookshelves and books. Two of the bedrooms overlooked the back yard, but the largest—*plus* the sitting area—opened out onto a balcony that had a lovely view of the ocean.

Amber had always thought her aunt's house to be very nice, but as she showed the agent around she noticed for the first time that the décor was rather dated, and some of the furniture a little shabby. The lace curtains in the bedrooms looked old-fashioned, and, whilst the polished wooden floors were okay, the patterned rugs that covered them were not.

Perhaps she'd become used to living in Warwick's super-modern, super-stylish apartment, with its wall-to-wall cream carpet, slick new furniture, recessed lighting and shiny surfaces. Whatever, she suddenly saw that her aunt's place could do with some modernising. As she showed Jim around Amber began making mental notes on what she would do to the property, if she stayed on. The multicoloured walls would all be painted cream. Out would go the myriad lace curtains and in would come cream plantation shutters. The floral bedding needed replacing with something more modern, as did the overly patterned rugs. The bathrooms, fortunately, were fine, being all white. But there were far too many knick-knacks cluttering every available surface. Most of these could go to a charity shop.

Even the comfy country kitchen required some attention. The pine cupboards were okay but some granite bench tops would give the room a real lift, as would a tiled floor. There really was way too much wood.

Her head was buzzing with plans by the time the tour was over.

'I probably will sell eventually,' Amber told Jim as she escorted him out onto the back porch. 'But not just yet. I don't think I'd get the best price, the way the house is presented at the moment.' She also wanted a project that would keep her mind occupied for the next few weeks, something to distract her from the depression that was sure to descend, now that all her secret hopes and dreams for the future with Warwick were dashed.

'You're quite right,' Jim agreed. 'You would achieve

a better price with some changes. The décor spells out old lady, whereas the buyer prepared to pay top dollar for this place would be a young professional couple with a family looking for a holiday home which they could let out as well.

'Though to be honest, Amber,' he went on without drawing breath, 'there are always buyers for homes in this location, regardless of their condition and presentation. I could get you a million for this place tomorrow without your having to spend a cent. Let me warn you that changing things takes time. Time and money.'

'True. But the real-estate market is picking up at the moment from what I've heard.' She hadn't gone to countless dinners with all those wheeler-dealer contacts of Warwick's without learning something. 'And any beachside property sells for more during the spring and summer months. It would be far more sensible of me to fix this place up a bit, then put it on the market in a couple of months time.'

'Wow,' Jim said. 'Not only beautiful but brainy as well.'

Amber just smiled.

'I have your card,' she said politely. 'I'll contact you if and when I'm ready to sell.'

'You mean you might not sell at all?'

'I don't believe in making rash decisions.' She'd only done that once, and look where it had got her?

'Sensible girl. Look, I hope you won't think I'm being pushy, but would you like to go out to dinner tonight?'

Amber blinked her surprise. She'd forgotten how aggressive some men could be in their pursuit of the fairer sex. In the ten months she'd lived with Warwick, none of his male acquaintances had ever hit on her. But that was because they wouldn't have dared.

Now, however, she was single again, and living alone, with no one to protect her from unwanted advances.

'I noticed when you were making me coffee earlier that there wasn't much in the way of food in the kitchen cupboards,' Jim went on before she could open her mouth. 'There's several great restaurants in Terrigal. We could do French, or Mexican, or seafood. Whatever you fancy.'

Amber knew full well that it wasn't concern for her lack of food that had inspired that invitation, but the predatorial gleam in his eyes that she'd glimpsed every now and then. The last thing she wanted at the moment was to fend off some testosterone-laden thirty-year-old who thought he was God's gift to women.

Which Jim Hansen obviously did.

No doubt Jim was a great success in his job. Warwick would not have rung that particular agent without having found out through one of his many business contacts who on the Central Coast had sold the most houses last year. Given Jim's natural good looks and confident manner, he was also no doubt a great success with the opposite sex.

But he was fighting a losing battle with her. Amber wanted nothing to do with men for a long, long time.

'Thank you for the offer, Jim,' she said. 'It's very kind of you. But I am dining with some friends tonight who live not far from here.' Of course it was a lie, but only a little white one. Amber had never been the sort of girl to issue brutal rejections.

He did look disappointed. And perhaps a little surprised. Clearly, he was no more used to rejection than Warwick.

Damn it, she'd been trying not to think about *him*.

Jim recovered quickly. 'I'll ask again, you know.'

This time, Amber gave him a firm look. 'Please don't. You'll be wasting your time.'

'You already have a boyfriend, is that it?'

'I did. Till recently. And I don't want another right now.'

'Understood,' he replied, but with a smug little smile hovering around his lips. 'Call me if you need anything. Anything at all.'

'I will,' she lied again. No way would she be calling Jim Hansen, even if she decided to sell tomorrow. She'd find a female agent who wouldn't give her any hassles. 'Thank you for calling,' she finished up coolly, hoping that he would finally get the message.

She stood there and watched him stride over to his car, a shiny black sporty number with HANSEN spelt out on the black and white number plate. Not a Ferrari, but it looked expensive just the same. He gave her a wave and another smile as he climbed in.

Amber returned the wave but not the smile.

Just go, she thought irritably.

He did. Eventually. Though he took his time.

Amber sighed her relief once the black car disappeared up the street. And to think she'd *wanted* his company earlier.

The sun suddenly going behind a cloud sent a shiver running down her spine. Crossing her arms, Amber had just turned to go back inside when she heard a decidedly familiar sound. The noise a Ferrari made when throttling down was unlike any other sound.

She spun back round, her mouth falling open as Warwick swung his car into the driveway in much the same way as he'd left earlier. After accelerating into the back yard at a ridiculous speed, he did a U-turn across the lawn and screeched to a halt in the same space Jim Hansen's car had occupied a few seconds earlier.

This time, Amber's immediate and only reaction to Warwick's return was shock. Down deep, she'd been absolutely certain that he would not come back. He was out of the car in a flash, his face darkly frustrated as he marched around the front and over to her.

'I was beginning to think I'd have to come inside and throw that idiot out,' he ground out. 'What in hell were you doing with Hansen that took so long? Or shouldn't I ask?'

Amber's mouth finally snapped shut, her shock giving way to outrage.

'No! You *shouldn't* ask. What I do with Jim Hansen, or any other man, is none of your business. We're finished. *Remember?*'

'We're finished when I say we're finished, madam. And that's certainly not today. Now, do you want to argue out here where all the neighbours can hear? Or shall we go inside where we can talk like reasonable adults?'

He didn't wait for her to answer, cupping her right elbow with steel-like fingers and steering her firmly back inside through the open door. Once in the hallway, he kicked the door shut, then took hold of both her shoulders, forcing her to look up into his angry blue eyes.

'I'm going to ask you one more time, Amber. What took you so bloody long with that oily-looking person?'

'I don't know what you're so upset about. You're the one who arranged for Jim to call.'

'So it's Jim already, is it?'

'And why not? We don't stand on ceremony here in Australia. We get on a first-name basis pretty quickly. I would have thought a man as smart as yourself would have noticed our easy-going Aussie culture by now.'

'Very funny. Have you asked Hansen to sell the house?'

'Not as yet. I've decided to live here for a while.'

'Really. If that's the case, then I wonder why our esteemed estate agent left here with that Cheshire Cat grin on his face. Still, it doesn't take a genius to work out the reason behind his smugness. Given the amount of time you spent with him, he probably thought he was on to a sure thing.'

'Oh, for pity's sake!' Amber wrenched herself out of Warwick's almost painful grip and marched into the nearby kitchen where she was able to put the table between herself and Warwick. Not to protect herself from him, but because she wanted to hit him more than she'd wanted to hit anyone in her life.

He followed her, his body language that of a man struggling with some suppressed violence of his own.

'Hansen asked you out, didn't he?' he bit out as he gripped the back of one of the wooden chairs with whitened knuckles.

Why, oh, why did she have to look guilty?

'What's it to you if he did?' she threw at him in desperate defiance. 'You don't want me. Not really. You were going to break up with me. The only reason you're here now creating a fuss is because your precious ego's been bruised.'

His hands curled into furious fists as they dropped to his side. 'I'm warning you, Amber.'

She drew herself up to her full height, her chin lifting. 'I'm not afraid of you, Warwick Kincaid.'

'You should be. As for my not wanting you, you're very wrong about that. I do want you, Amber, more than ever. Now tell me that you haven't agreed to go out with Hansen.'

Amber stared at him. Goodness, he was jealous! Blackly, insanely jealous! That was why he wanted her more than ever. Not because he'd realised he was in love with her, but because some other man was showing interest in her.

'*Tell* me,' he repeated in ominous tones.

Her temper rose to a level previously unknown to her. 'Don't you dare try to bully me, Warwick Kincaid. I don't have to tell you anything of the kind. You don't own me!'

'Don't I? We'll just see about that!'

He was around the table in a split second, coming at her with burning eyes. Amber did the only thing she could think of to do. She shoved a chair into his shins and ran. Unfortunately, not out the back door, which would have been the more sensible escape. But up the stairs where the only barriers to being caught were the less-than-adequate locks on the bedroom doors.

Behind her she heard him coming. Fast. Her heart hammered hard in her chest as total panic set in. What was he going to do? Warwick could be a ruthless seducer when he wanted to be. But he'd never forced her to do anything she didn't ultimately want to do, even when she hadn't initially wanted to do it, like last night.

Was that his plan now? To show her that she had no power against him once she was in his arms?

But if he succeeded in seducing her, she would be left with nothing, not even her pride...

Suddenly, Amber's rushing feet clipped the edge of the slightly higher top step, sending her sprawling onto the thin strip of patterned carpet that ran along the upstairs hallway. Before she had time to get up, he'd reached her.

'Are you all right?' he asked as he lifted her, his voice as perversely gentle as the hands encircling her waist.

'You keep away from me!' she screamed, wrenching out of his arms and pushing him away quite violently.

He crashed back against the wall, grunting with pain. For a split second Amber just stood there, staring at him. But as soon as he levered himself away from the wall, she came to her senses and made a second dash for it, this time down the stairs, thinking if she could only make it outside she'd be safe.

She almost made it. Speed, however, was her undoing once more, not helped by the shiny soles of her nice new boots. Halfway down the stairs, her left foot shot out from under her, her right leg buckling when she tried to take all her weight on her right foot. It was then that she tipped forward, and the hallway floor rushed up to meet her...

CHAPTER EIGHT

'OH, MY God!' Warwick cried out.

He couldn't save her. It all happened too fast.

Warwick would never forget the horrible sound Amber's head made when it hit the floor at the bottom of the stairs, or the way she lay, in a crumpled heap. Not moving, maybe not breathing.

She's dead, came the horrifying thought as he raced down the stairs, his own heart almost stopping as he knelt beside her still body and tried to find her pulse.

'Please don't let her be dead,' he prayed for the first time in his life.

When her eyelashes fluttered and a soft moan escaped her lips, his heart lurched back to life, his relief almost as great as his guilt.

Because her falling was all his fault. What had he thought he was doing, threatening her like that, then chasing her up the stairs? No wonder she'd panicked. He'd obviously scared her.

So much for his earlier plan to return and play the role of the penitent lover, all apologies and kisses. Instead, as he'd sat outside in the street, waiting for Hansen to leave, he'd fairly seethed with uncontrollable jealousy. Because once he'd seen that black sports car with the personalised number plate, he'd known what kind of man

Jim Hansen would be. He knew the type well. When he'd spotted the handsome devil driving out with that smug smile on his face, he'd come roaring back inside like some Neanderthal caveman, his primal emotions bypassing his brain as he'd tried to get his way through sheer brute force.

Aside from the fact that he deplored that kind of macho behaviour, such tactics simply didn't work with the modern woman. You couldn't hit her on the head with a club, then drag her off to your cave and ravish her for hours.

Not without ending up in jail.

He deserved to be in jail. Or in hell.

Damn it all, he *was* in hell!

'I'm so sorry,' he groaned as he tried to work out what to do first. 'So terribly terribly sorry.'

When he started sliding his arms underneath her body, her eyelids shot up. 'Don't you touch me!' she cried out, eyes and voice alarmed.

'Don't be silly. You can't stay here on the floor. We have to get you onto a bed. Now where's the closest?'

'No!'

'For pity's sake, I'm not going to hurt you, Amber. What kind of man do you think I am?'

'I don't know,' she choked out. 'I don't know any more.' And she turned her face away from him. But not before he glimpsed tears filling her eyes.

Never in his life had Warwick felt so low, or so remorseful.

'I give you my word,' he said sincerely as he lifted her up into his arms, 'that I won't do anything more to upset you.'

Her eyes turned back to his then, haunted, unhappy eyes.

'What more could you possibly do, Warwick?'

How right she was. He'd reached new depths of reprehensible behaviour today, having had no consideration for Amber's feelings, having thought of no one but himself.

Of course he'd been treating women badly for years, using them to satisfy his own base needs, then discarding them when he'd grown bored with their wanting more from him than just sex. He'd justified his behaviour by selecting the sort of good-looking, gold-digging female who hadn't been too broken-hearted when he'd sent them off into the sunset loaded with jewellery and cars and the odd apartment or two.

He could never, however, justify what he'd done to Amber. She was just not like that.

He had to let her go. But first he had to make things right here. He couldn't just leave when she might have concussion and who knew what other injuries, all of which were his fault. The thought that she might have really hurt herself in that fall still appalled him.

'Amber, I—'

'No,' she interrupted, stiffening in his arms. 'I don't want to listen to anything more you've got to say. Just put me down and go.'

Warwick might have admired her spirit at any other time. But he could hardly do what she wanted and still live with himself.

'Please understand, Amber, that I can't do that,' he said firmly. 'Firstly you might have concussion after a bad fall like that. Secondly, I think you could have broken something.'

'I haven't done any such thing. Here. Put me down and I'll show you.'

He sighed when she began to struggle. Silly stubborn girl! In the end, it was easier to lower her to the floor—very gingerly—and let her try to stand up.

Her gasp of pain, plus the awful shade of grey to which her face turned, showed him that he was right. She'd broken something all right.

'I…I think…my ankle,' she said weakly as she tried to balance on her left leg, at the same time clutching at his arm. 'I think I will have to lie down. Aunt Kate's bedroom is just over there,' she said, biting her bottom lip as she nodded towards a doorway across the hall. 'Oh…I…I…'

He caught her this time before she hit the floor, scooping her limp body up into his arms and hurrying into the bedroom she'd indicated.

It was a truly ghastly bedroom, in Warwick's opinion, all dark wooden furniture with lace everywhere and the most hideous crocheted bedspread he'd ever seen.

He lowered Amber onto said bedspread, trying not to worry too much. She'd just fainted, that was all. No one died from fainting. He wondered if he should cover her with a blanket. It was quite chilly inside the house. Whatever heating there was clearly wasn't on. Not wanting to move her, he reefed the bedspread out from the foot of the bed and turned it back up over her legs. By the time he glanced back up at her face, her eyes were open.

'I fainted,' she said, as though it were a crime.

'Yes,' he agreed.

'I've never fainted before.'

His smile was gentle as he sat beside her on the bed. 'Possibly because you've never broken an ankle before. I have and it's not a very pleasant experience.'

'You have? When?'

'A few years back. An abseiling accident.'

'Abseiling,' she repeated drily, and shook her head at him. 'What haven't you done, Warwick?'

'I haven't tried base jumping,' he said, pleased to see the colour coming back into her face. 'Now first things first. Are you in a lot of pain?'

'Not so much now that I'm lying down. My ankle's throbbing a bit and I have a headache. Nothing I can't stand.'

'But why should you stand it? Your aunt must have kept some painkillers. Where did she store her medicines? Over there, in that bathroom?'

'No. In the kitchen. In the cupboard above the fridge.'

'I'll go and check. Now don't go trying to get up, madam,' he warned as he stood up. 'I don't want to come back here and find you on the floor.' Warwick grimaced when he glanced down at the ancient, dusty rug by the bed. 'Certainly not this floor. The mites in that rug just might have you for lunch!'

Amber did try to move once he'd left the room. But the pain was too awful to continue. There was nothing she could do but lie back and let Warwick minister to her. Which was the last thing she wanted.

Possibly it was the last thing he wanted as well. Warwick was not the sort of man who would enjoy playing Florence Nightingale. He was used to being waited on, not the other way around.

If only he hadn't come back. If only she'd never met him in the first place!

Life was cruel all right.

He returned quite quickly with a glass of water and two white tablets.

'I found some strong painkillers,' he said and popped

the tablets into her hand. 'You're not allergic to codeine, are you?'

'No,' she said, and swallowed the tablets, drinking most of the water with them.

'Right. I've been thinking. We'll have to find a doctor who'll call here at the house. No way can I get you into the Ferrari with a broken ankle. So who shall we call? What about your aunt Kate's doctor? She must have had a GP, having lived up here for so long.'

'I have some bad news for you, Warwick. Doctors don't make house calls on the coast.'

'What? Not even family doctors?'

'No, not even family doctors.'

He looked decidedly sceptical. 'Why not?'

'Because there aren't enough of them to go around as it is. I think you'll find the situation is pretty much the same all over Australia. We have a major shortage of medical staff in this country. You've been lucky not to have been sick since you came here, or to have fallen off any of those stupid mountains you climb and ski down.'

'So what do you do if you have an accident?'

'You either drive yourself to the emergency section of the local hospital, where, because of the lack of doctors and nurses, it sometimes takes hours to be seen. Or you call an ambulance in the hope that when you arrive at that same place, you'll hopefully be seen a little more quickly. Though I wouldn't bank on it. Given I can't even walk, I think an ambulance is the best course of action.'

Warwick couldn't imagine anything worse than sitting for hours with Amber in an inadequately staffed emergency room, waiting to be treated.

There had to be some other solution.

And then it came to him: Max Richmond! He might never have met the hotel magnate, but he knew Max was both rich and successful, the kind of man who'd have connections.

'What about Max Richmond?' he asked Amber. 'Didn't you say he lived not far from here? You told me that he and his wife were close friends of your aunt Kate.'

'Well, yes, but I don't think that—'

'Do you have his phone number?' Warwick interrupted.

'Yes, but—'

'But nothing, Amber. I'm not having you sit around in some hospital waiting room for hours. Max Richmond is sure to know a local doctor who'd be willing to make a house call, for a price. After that we can organise to have you taken to a private hospital. What's his number?' he asked as he pulled his phone out of his trouser pocket.

He was doing it again, Amber realised wearily. Taking over. It was what he did best, of course. But the days of his taking her over were over. She'd found the courage to leave him today, and, despite it breaking her heart, she knew she could not let him seduce her back into his life in any way, shape or form. She had to stand on her own two feet, even if she had a broken ankle.

'Warwick,' she said, after counting to ten.

'What is it?'

'I don't know Max Richmond's number off by heart and I wouldn't give it to you, even if I did. Now please… ring an ambulance for me.'

He didn't say or do anything for several seconds, but just frowned. But then he nodded with what she hoped was acceptance.

'If that's what you really want me to do.'

'It's what I really want you to do,' she repeated. 'And make it sound like an emergency, otherwise they'll take ages to come. You can do that for me, can't you?'

'Lie, you mean?'

'Just exaggerate a bit.'

'Sure.' And he did, quite brilliantly.

'They'll be here shortly,' he said after he'd completed the call.

'Good,' she said. 'Then, after they've taken me to hospital, I want you to drive back to Sydney and never contact me again.'

She saw the flash of anger in his eyes. Or was it distress? No, no, it had to be anger.

'I won't be leaving you, Amber,' he said. 'Not till I know you're going to be all right. Don't ask that of me.'

She sighed her exasperation, not just at him but herself, for feeling some pleasure at his refusing to go.

'What's the point of your staying?' she said frustratedly. 'We're finished. You know that as well as I do. It was cruel of you to come back today at all. Why did you, for pity's sake? Why couldn't you have let things be?'

He sighed. 'I wish I had. Now.'

He did, indeed, look regretful.

'It was a mistake,' he added.

She could not trust herself to answer that, knowing that she was close to crying. And she didn't want to cry. Not after he'd virtually called her a cry baby. No more tears, she lectured herself, no more weak, silly, soppy tears!

'I'm really sorry, Amber,' he said. 'I never meant to hurt you.'

This time, it wasn't tears that filled her eyes but fury.

'No kidding!' she snapped. 'What did you mean to do today, then?'

He just stared at her for a long time with bleak eyes.

Suddenly, she realised she didn't want their relationship to end without telling him the truth.

'I was never going to say this to you, Warwick, but the time has come.'

'Say what?'

'That I love you.'

'Amber...please don't do this,' he said with a grimace.

'It's all right. I'm not going to make a fuss. I just wanted to tell you the way it is. I admit I didn't love you at first. How could I? I didn't even know you. But somewhere along the line—quite soon, I think—I fell in love with you. I'm not sure why. Love, I've come to realise, doesn't always make sense. But you know what? One day in the future, after I've managed to get you out of my system, I'll fall in love with someone else, because that's what I want to do with my life. Whereas you'll just continue doing what you've always done: going from woman to woman, living for nothing but the pleasure of the moment. Till one day you'll suddenly wake up and find that you're a very bored, very lonely old man.'

Warwick's heart squeezed tight in his chest at her declaration of love. He found it strange that hearing Amber say the actual words was much more affecting than he'd have thought. As far as the rest of what she said... He didn't doubt she was quite right. Except in her prediction of his becoming a lonely old man. He would make sure the old part would never happen. As for his being lonely. The truth was he was already lonely. He'd always been lonely, for as long as he could remember.

Only with Amber had he felt less alone. And less… unloved.

That was what she'd given him that he couldn't resist.

Love.

That was why he was having such difficulty in ending their relationship.

But it has to be done, doesn't it, Warwick?

For her sake.

'You're absolutely right,' he said. 'I'm a cold, unfeeling bastard and I have no idea why you would love me. Still, I'm pleased to know that you do want to fall in love again at some stage. Just not with Jim Hansen, please,' he added drily.

'It won't be Jim Hansen. If you must know I can't stand the man.'

'I am relieved.'

Amber rolled her eyes. 'Might I remind you you were the one who contacted him?'

'Yes, but that was when I thought I'd be with you. He wouldn't have dared make a move on you if I'd been around.'

'I can look after myself, Warwick.'

'I hope so.'

'Did you worry about your other dumped mistresses this much?'

'No. But that's because they were real mistresses. You, dearest Amber, were my live-in girlfriend, whom I will continue to worry about until I know you are fit and able to look after yourself properly. So I'm afraid you'll have to tolerate my following the ambulance to the hospital and making sure you're being well taken care of. After all, you can't stop me, can you?' he added, a touch smugly.

Amber was torn between exasperation and resignation.

'I suppose I can't,' she said grudgingly. 'But don't think I'm going back to Sydney with you at any stage, because I won't.'

'I wouldn't ask that of you,' came his honest reply.

She looked surprised by his answer. And just a tiny bit disappointed. She was still in love with him, Warwick realised.

It was a very corrupting thought.

So don't think about it!

The sound of a vehicle pulling into the yard was a welcome distraction.

'That'll be the ambulance,' he said. 'I'll go meet them, tell them you've regained consciousness.'

Amber shook her head at him. 'You are a wicked man, Warwick Kincaid.'

CHAPTER NINE

I wish I were, Warwick thought as he strode from the room. A wicked man would lie and tell Amber that he loved her too, then ask her to marry him. A truly wicked man might even tell her the truth about himself, taking advantage of her compassionate heart so that he'd have a loving carer when the inevitable finally happened.

'Looks like you're not as wicked as you've always thought you were,' he muttered to himself under his breath as he exited the house.

In the end, Warwick didn't follow the ambulance into Gosford, the paramedics informing him that the rest of the afternoon would be taken up with X-rays or scans and he would just be in the way. They suggested he went in during visiting hours that evening, by which time Amber would have a diagnosis. In the meantime, she did have her cell phone with her so she could ring him if she needed to.

Warwick had no doubt that if Amber's ankle was broken, they would operate. They did that these days, the theory being that strengthening the ankle with steel pins would save the patient from arthritis later in life. A rather wasted prevention where he'd been concerned. But he'd still chosen the operation, because recovery was quicker and you could get around better by wearing a special boot and using a walking frame. Much more convenient that a cast and crutches.

Warwick's only concern was who would perform Amber's operation. He'd had one of the best bone men in the world do his, after which he'd convalesced in a private sanatorium in Switzerland, where he'd been waited on hand and foot. He didn't like the idea of Amber being operated on by some second-rate surgeon, then being tossed out of hospital within a day or two without proper after-care. What he needed to do before visiting Amber tonight was to find out about the best private hospitals in the area, plus the qualifications of the specialists who operated there.

After the ambulance departed, Warwick remained out on the still sunny and almost warm porch whilst he thought about how best he could glean this information, and how quickly. If he'd had a lot of time he'd have contacted his office in London, where his top research assistant could find all the answers he wanted via the worldwide web. His staff there were highly efficient and quite ingenious. But searching the Internet would still take some time. A glance at his watch showed it was getting on for four o'clock. Why do that when there was a local and more immediate source of information?

Turning, Warwick hurried back inside and into the decidedly chilly kitchen where he spotted a phone on one of the kitchen counters and a telephone and address book sitting beside it. He quickly turned to the R section and there it was: Max and Tara Richmond's phone number. First he put the number into the menu of his BlackBerry, then he called.

'Hello,' a female voice answered quite quickly.

'Mrs Richmond?'

'Yes. Who is this?' she asked a little irritably.

She probably thought he was a telemarketer. 'You don't know me personally, Mrs Richmond. My name is Warwick Kincaid. I'm a friend of Amber Roberts, Kate's niece.'

'Ah, yes! Mr Kincaid. I know who you are. Kate mentioned you to us once or twice.'

'Not with any great approval, I would imagine,' he said drily. 'But that's beside the point now. The thing is, Mrs Richmond—'

'Oh, do call me Tara. I can't stand being called Mrs Richmond.'

'Very well, Tara.'

'I suppose you're ringing for the solicitor's name and address.'

'What? No. No, that's not why I'm phoning.'

'Didn't Mrs Roberts pass on my message?'

'What message?'

'That Kate used our solicitor to make her will. He wants Amber to contact him.'

'I see. Well, I'm not sure about that. Amber didn't mention it to me. But that's not important at the moment. The thing is, Tara, there's been an accident at the house. Kate's B & B, that is. When we heard about Amber's inheritance, we came up from Sydney for the day to look at the place. Unfortunately, Amber tripped and fell down the stairs and I'm pretty sure she's broken her ankle.'

'Oh, dear heaven, how dreadful. Have you called an ambulance?'

'Yes. It's just left here to take her to Gosford hospital.'

'I see. So how can I help?'

'Amber explained to me about the shortage of doctors and I am quite concerned about who is going to treat her. As you can understand, I want the very best for her, so I was wondering if you or your husband could advise me as to which private hospital I could have her transferred to?'

'Mmm. Well, there are a few private hospitals on the coast. But I couldn't personally recommend any particular one, because I've never been to any of them, and neither has Max. I actually had my two babies in Gosford hospital, where I was treated wonderfully well. You shouldn't believe everything you read, you know. There are good and bad everywhere. And you'll find that the specialists at Gosford hospital also practise locally in the private sector.'

'Really? The system appears to be just the same here as it is at home in the UK.'

'I wouldn't worry about her standard of care, if I were you. She'll be just fine. Poor thing, though. It's nasty, breaking an ankle. It's going to take weeks before she can walk properly again. I hope your place in Sydney doesn't have stairs.'

'It doesn't.' Not that Amber would be there. But it did beg the question of where she would convalesce. She couldn't stay by herself at her aunt's place. Well, she *could*, if she allowed him to pay for a private nurse to come in every day. But Warwick couldn't see her letting him pay for anything. He supposed she'd have to go home to her family. She wasn't going to like that!

'It just occurred to me,' Tara said. 'If you are only up here for the day, then Amber won't have anything with her for a stay in hospital. No toilet bag or nighties.'

'Well…no. She didn't have anything like that with her.'

'I'd send you out to shop for her, but if you're anything like Max you won't know what to buy. I'd go myself but Jasmine's having her afternoon nap. Why don't I put some things together for you to take in to her? I have nighties I haven't even worn and we have loads of sample toiletries which people try to sell to Max for his hotel chain.'

'That's extremely kind of you,' he said, and meant it.

'No trouble. When do you think you'll be going in to the hospital?'

'The paramedics said not to bother until tonight. By then, Amber should have been X-rayed and we'll know what the situation is.'

'Right. I presume you're ringing from Kate's place?'

'Yes.'

'Okay. Look, Max goes for a jog along the beach every afternoon around five. Our house is only a couple of minutes from you, so I'll send him along with a bag of things.'

'Are you sure? I could always drive to your place and collect it. It's obviously not far.'

'Don't be silly. It's not out of Max's way. He won't mind.'

'I do thank you. And I'm sure Amber will be most grateful.'

'Only too glad to help. She's a lovely girl.'

'Yes. Yes, she is.'

'Give her my best wishes and do let me know what happens. With a bit of luck her ankle might not be broken, only sprained.'

'Let's hope so. Anyway, I'll ring you when I know the diagnosis.'

'Great. Bye,' she said, then hung up.

Warwick glanced at his watch again. Ten past four.

Suddenly, he felt hungry. And damned cold. This kitchen was rapidly becoming an ice-box. He was used to places that were fully temperature-controlled all the time. He hadn't even brought a jacket with him. He spotted Amber's leather jacket draped over the back of a chair but he could hardly wear that. He found a small fan heater in one corner and turned it on, then set about getting himself something to eat.

There were quite a lot of tins in the cupboards and various loaves of bread in the freezer. He made himself some raisin toast and coffee, which he consumed in record time, after which he decided to have a quick look around the house. When he'd been up here for that barbecue at Easter, he'd only come inside once to go to the small washroom under the stairs. Today was the first time he'd been in the kitchen. Certainly the first time he'd been in the old lady's bedroom.

A brief glance into the formal lounge and dining room showed more dark wooden furniture, which some people might think elegant and timeless, but it wasn't to Warwick's taste. Warwick preferred modern and minimalist furniture, hating anything fussy.

Finally he went back upstairs, this time more slowly, and was surprised when he discovered some temperature controls built into the wall at the top of the staircase, indicating that the upstairs *was* air conditioned. He didn't turn it on, however, fully intending to drive back to Sydney after visiting Amber. No way was he going to stay here tonight. Not if all the bedrooms looked and smelled like the one downstairs; lavender and lace were not to his liking!

The bedrooms upstairs, however, came as a pleasant surprise. They weren't at all bad. There wasn't quite so much lace as downstairs, as it was hung only at the windows. And there was no overpowering smell of lavender. He particularly liked the largest bedroom, which had a queen-sized bed, an en suite bathroom, and French doors opening out onto an ocean-facing balcony. Admittedly the décor was still a bit too old-fashioned for his taste—he hated floral quilts and rugs—but he could ignore those.

Maybe he wouldn't drive back to Sydney tonight after all…

Unlocking the French doors, he pushed them open and walked out onto the balcony where a crisp evening breeze sent the scent of the ocean into his nostrils.

Warwick had always liked the sea. He liked the sound of the waves washing up onto the beach, savoured the sharp, salty smell.

That was one memory from his childhood that he still found pleasure in: his summers by the sea.

When he'd been around eight years old, his father had bought a holiday house right on the coast in Cornwall, in a village that boasted one of the best beaches in England. Not that his father had spent much time there. It had mostly just been Warwick and the housekeeper who'd acted as his minder during the holidays. She'd been a very large lady named Phyllis, who'd drunk like a fish and let Warwick pretty well do whatever he liked. He'd spent each summer playing and swimming with the local children, who'd also taught him how to fish and even to ride a surfboard. He'd absolutely loved it, hating it when the holidays were over and he'd had to return to boarding school.

Unfortunately, when Warwick had turned twelve, his father had sold the Cornish house. After that, his summer holidays had been spent in various camps that specialised in teaching adolescent boys how to survive in the wild. He'd hated them, perhaps because his heart had stayed on the beach in Cornwall. He still hated any form of camping, which was perverse given he liked the great outdoors—just not in a tent, thank you very much, or a dank forest.

Nothing beat holidays by the ocean.

In the summer, that is, Warwick amended as a shiver went through him. Not quite so great in the winter time. Especially when one didn't have a warm jacket to wear. Warwick was about to go back inside when he spotted a tall, well-built man jogging along the beach, carrying a sports bag with him. It had to be Richmond, despite it not being five o'clock just yet. Warwick watched as the man made his way across the sand to the street that ran along the lakefront, where he briefly disappeared from view behind neighbouring houses.

Knowing it wouldn't take him long to arrive, Warwick hurried downstairs and along the hallway to the back door, opening it just as the hotel magnate ran into the back yard.

Not that he looked like a hotel magnate. He was dressed in navy track pants and a grey windcheater, and Richmond's close-cut hairstyle and unshaven face projected a tougher, more physical image than Warwick might have expected. As he drew closer, however, he could see the intelligence in Richmond's eyes. And something else…

Disapproval.

'Tara sent these over for Amber,' he said rather abruptly as he handed over the bag.

Clearly, Max Richmond had preconceived ideas about Warwick's character, none of which was good.

Warwick did not blame the man for thinking he was a cad. Because he was. But he was also a gentlemanly cad. If there was one good thing his father had taught him, it was manners.

'It was very kind of her to do that,' Warwick said politely. 'And very good of you to bring them by. Thank you. I'm Warwick Kincaid, by the way.' And he held out his right hand.

Richmond hesitated only briefly before taking his hand and shaking it. 'Max Richmond,' he replied. 'So how is Amber? Are you sure her ankle's broken?'

'Not absolutely. But she can't put any weight on it at all. I should find out for sure when I visit her at the hospital tonight.'

'Let us know, will you? Tara's quite worried about her.'

'I'll do that. And thank your wife again for me, will you?'

'Sure thing. Bye,' he said, a little more warmly than when he arrived.

Warwick watched Max jog off before carrying the bag inside the increasingly cold house. Cold and dark. Turning on the hall light, he closed the door and glanced up the stairs. Should he go up there and turn on the heating? Or should he just get out of here and find somewhere warm and comfortable to have a meal before going to the hospital to visit Amber?

Amber…

A bleak wave of guilt washed through Warwick as his mind returned to Amber. It was no wonder people held a bad opinion of him.

'Shame on you,' her aunt had said to him, only a few yards from where he was standing at this moment.

What would she have said if she'd seen the way he'd acted today? He deserved to be tarred and feathered for chasing after Amber like that. For making her afraid. For making her fall.

And now, because of him, she was in hospital, all alone.

There was no one in there with her, holding her hand. No one to reassure her that everything would be all right, no one at all.

Not that Amber wanted him in there holding her hand. He was good for nothing in her opinion. Which wasn't totally true, Warwick thought a tad caustically. He *was* good for looking after her financially, if she'd let him.

By the time Warwick locked up and left the house for the drive into Gosford, he vowed to do everything in his power to persuade Amber to accept his help with her convalescence. Considering she'd been going to accept a five-million-dollar apartment, surely she'd accept a few measly thousand towards paying for a private nurse.

Warwick could not possibly have anticipated that fate would present another alternative for Amber's convalescence, one that would tempt him anew, then test him to the nth degree...

CHAPTER TEN

WITHIN one minute of her mother having answered the phone, Amber was regretting making the call. She'd been feeling terribly low and a little frightened as she'd never been in hospital before, let alone been faced with an operation. On top of that, the evening's visiting hours had begun, and Warwick hadn't arrived. The other three patients in the ward, however, all had visitors, making her feel unloved and horribly alone.

It had seemed the natural thing to do to ring home and tell her parents about her broken ankle. When her mother sounded genuinely concerned and sympathetic, Amber even momentarily considered telling her that she'd split up with Warwick.

Till she realised what she would be setting herself up for.

'I'll be fine, Mum, honest,' Amber said, squeezing her eyes shut in frustration. Why, oh, why hadn't she foreseen how her mother might react to her news? 'The doctor said the operation's a very simple one. And that I'll be out of hospital the day after tomorrow. There's absolutely no need for you to drive all the way up here.'

'But what about when you leave the hospital? How will you cope?'

'I'll be fine, Mum. Warwick will look after me.'

'Hmph!' Doreen snorted. 'I know exactly what he'll do. Hire some snooty nurse to stay home with you in that fancy apartment of his whilst he swans off, looking for mistress number twenty-five! No, no, my girl, you'll be coming home here where you can be looked after properly.'

Full-on panic set in. She wasn't going to go home, no way!

'You are so wrong about Warwick, Mum,' Amber defended in desperation. 'He's already offered to look after me personally. And not in his apartment. We're going to be staying up here in Aunt Kate's place.'

'Don't be ridiculous!' Doreen exclaimed. 'That place has stairs—steep ones! You should know that since you fell down them today.'

'I don't need to go upstairs,' Amber pointed out. 'I can sleep in Aunt Kate's bedroom. It has a bathroom attached, a TV and everything else I could possibly need.'

'Oh, yes. I'd forgotten about that room,' Doreen said grudgingly. 'But what about meals? I can't see Warwick Kincaid being able to cook.'

'Of course he can cook. Warwick can do anything he sets his mind to,' Amber added, sucking in sharply when she opened her eyes to find the man himself standing at the foot of her hospital bed with a frown on his handsome face.

Amber winced at the realisation that he must have overheard at least some of her outrageous lies. Still, she'd straighten everything out with him when she finally got off the phone. In the meantime she had to prevent her mother from driving up and seeing for herself that her relationship with Warwick was over.

'What about your washing?' Doreen kept on with

relentless logic. 'I'll bet he's never operated a washing machine in his life.'

'One doesn't have to be a genius to operate a washing machine, Mum.'

'You don't want my help,' Doreen replied, sounding rather wan all of a sudden. 'Do you?'

Now Amber felt guilty. 'It's not that, Mum. But I'm not a child any longer. I have to learn to cope with my own problems.'

Her mother sighed. 'You will ask, if you ever need me, won't you?'

'Yes, yes, of course I will.'

'It's not that far to Wamberal, you know. I could drive up during the day and still be back by the time your father gets home from work.'

Which would be the extent of her help if I stay up here, Amber thought bitterly. No way would she offer to leave everyone down there and stay with me for the next few weeks. That would mean putting me first for once. Couldn't do that, could you, Mum?

'Must go, Mum,' she said a bit abruptly. 'Warwick's just arrived.'

Another sigh wafted down the line.

'I hope everything goes well tomorrow, dear,' she said. 'I...I'll be in touch.' And she hung up.

'What was all that about my offering to look after you personally?' Warwick asked immediately.

Amber didn't see any point in lying. Clearly, he'd overheard everything.

'Mum wants me to go home with her after the operation,' she said with a weary sigh. 'As you can imagine, I don't want to, so I said you were going to look after me.'

'Right down to doing all the cooking and washing?' he said, sounding almost amused.

Amber shrugged. 'Yes, well, she máde some crack about you hiring a snooty nurse to stay with me in your fancy apartment whilst you…er…um…' Amber broke off, suddenly realising that he couldn't have overheard her mother's part of the conversation. So there was no need for her to be *that* honest.

'Whilst I what?' he demanded to know in that un-compromising way he had at times.

Amber finally decided that honesty *was* probably best after all.

'Whilst you were out looking for your next mistress,' she told him bluntly.

'Charming,' Warwick bit out. 'Absolutely charming.'

Amber found his condemnation of her mother's words somewhat hypocritical. 'You can't blame her for think-ing that.'

'I don't. But don't blame me if I find everyone's poor opinion of my character just a fraction irritating.'

'Who's everyone?'

'Max Richmond, for starters.'

'You met Max? How come?'

'Only very briefly. I found his number in your aunt's address book and rang to make some enquiries about private hospitals in this area. His wife answered and told me that they'd look after you just as well in this hospital. Not sure if I should have believed her,' he said, glancing with disapproval around the rather crowded four-bed ward. 'Are they looking after you?'

'I have no complaints. The food isn't so great but I'm not very hungry. Have you eaten?'

'I had a meal of sorts at a club not far from here. The Leagues' Club, I think it was called. I wasn't all that hungry, either. I was too worried about you. So what did the tests show? Is your ankle broken?'

'Yes, you were right. It's well and truly broken. They're going to operate first thing in the morning.'

'And the doctor? What did you think of him?'

'The nurses say he's very good. A top specialist who moved up from Sydney not long ago.'

'What's his name? I'll check him out.'

'You'll do no such thing,' Amber said sternly. 'Warwick, you have to stop this. I'm not your responsibility.'

'That's not the way I see it. I caused your accident, Amber. If it wasn't for my chasing you up those stairs and frightening the life out of you, you would never have fallen.'

'Please...I...I don't want to talk about that any more. What's done is done.'

Warwick hated seeing the vulnerability in her eyes, and the pain.

'So when will you be getting out?' he asked gently.

'The day after tomorrow.'

'Oh, I almost forgot,' he said, and lifted a bag up onto the foot of the bed. 'Tara Richmond sent some things for you. A couple of nighties and some toiletries. That's how I actually met Max Richmond. He brought them to the house.'

'That was very kind of her.'

'She sounded like a nice lady.'

'She is.'

'They asked me to let them know how you were.'

'Maybe I should give them a call,' Amber said, and picked up her phone once more.

'Can't you do it later?'

'No. No, I think I should do it now,' she said. 'I have their number in my phone. I was supposed to ring them anyway about seeing their solicitor. Something to do with Aunt Kate's will.'

Max tried not to feel put out whilst Amber called the Richmonds. He wasn't used to being less than number one with Amber. He certainly wasn't used to her looking at him in the way she'd looked at him a moment ago—as if he was no longer a part of her life.

Which he wasn't, of course.

Clearly it was Tara Richmond who answered Amber's phone call. The two women made girl-talk whilst Max wandered over to stare through the window by Amber's bed.

He wasn't looking at the town below. He was thinking.

Finally, he turned from the window and returned to the bed, just as Amber finished her chat with Tara.

'You didn't tell Tara or Max that we'd broken up,' she said straight away.

'You didn't tell your mother, either,' he countered.

'If I'd done that, she would have insisted I go home with her. This way, I can still be the boss of my own life.'

'You won't be able to manage on your own when you get out of hospital,' Warwick told her. 'I know that for a fact. You'll need someone with you all the time till you're properly healed.'

Amber hadn't thought that far ahead. Till now...

'I guess I'll have to pay someone,' she said.

'Private nursing costs a small fortune, Amber. I know you said you had money but you won't have much left in six weeks' time.'

'Six weeks!'

'That's how long it's going to take to mend.'

'I...I didn't realise...'

'Well, I do. So this is what I propose: I'll do exactly what you told your mother I was going to do. Look after you up here at your aunt's place till you get better. No, no, don't say a single word till I've finished. Initially, I was going to offer to pay for a private nurse to stay with you, but just now I realised that, even if you agreed, your mother would eventually find out what was going on and you'd have to tolerate all sorts of recriminations and criticisms, which you do not deserve. I know you're going to think I have a hidden agenda in making this amazingly generous offer. No doubt you'll imagine I'm just waiting my chance to have my wicked way with you again. But I give you my solemn word that that isn't the case. This is me doing what is right for once. This is me making amends for my totally selfish behaviour in the past. I want to look after you, Amber. Not as your lover but as a friend. There will be no sex. Then, when you're totally better, we'll part as friends. Not the way we parted today, in bitterness and anger. So what do you say? Will you trust me to do this for you?'

Amber just lay there, absolutely stunned. She found it difficult to know what to say. Because of course she wanted him to stay up here and look after her. It was a dream come true.

Though not quite. A dream come true would be his saying he was doing it because he loved her and could not bear to lose her. Amber knew that Warwick's amazingly generous gesture was inspired not by love but by guilt.

'I take it you're not too thrilled with my offer?' he asked.

'I'm just…surprised, that's all.'

Warwick's smile was wry. 'I can imagine. But you have only yourself to blame.'

'Me?'

'Yes. When I heard you telling your mother that I could do anything I set my mind to, I began thinking that maybe I *could*, even down to doing the cooking and washing. I admit it's going to be a challenge. But I'm game if you are.'

Down deep, Amber knew that to agree to what Warwick was proposing was probably not a good idea. But she didn't have the emotional—or the physical—strength to refuse. Today had been hell. Tomorrow didn't promise to be any better. Then there was the reality of how *would* she cope on her own?

Not very well.

'All right,' she said somewhat wearily. 'I accept your offer.'

'That's good. Now, before I forget, I need to know what you want me to collect for you from the apartment. I'm driving back down to Sydney tonight after I leave here. And before you tell me you don't want anything, just remember that you *will* need something to wear. You can't spend the next six weeks borrowing stuff from Tara. And you can hardly go shopping for more clothes just at the moment.'

Amber decided the time for excessive pride was not right now.

'Okay. But I don't want too much. Just some casual things, plus nightwear, undies and toiletries. Oh, and the towelling robe hanging on the back of the bathroom door.'

'Will do. Look, perhaps I'd better get going. What time is your operation tomorrow?'

'I'm one of the first in the morning. I can't drink or eat anything after midnight.'

'I'll ring the hospital mid-morning to find out how

things went and I'll be back to see you after lunch. You should be ready to face visitors by then. You're not allergic to anaesthetic or anything like that, are you?'

'I…I don't know,' she said, a bit shakily. 'Like I said, I've never had an operation before. I've always been disgustingly healthy.'

'In that case you'll be just fine,' he said, and bent forward to give her a peck on the forehead. 'Try to sleep, sweetheart. Oops. I mean, Amber.' He smiled as he straightened. 'Bad habits die hard. You might have to be patient with me. But I will do my level best to behave.'

'And to keep your hands off,' she reminded him.

He lifted his hands high into the air. 'You already have my solemn oath.'

Amber rolled her eyes. 'Oh, just go, for pity's sake, before I change my mind and tell you not to come back.'

'Methinks you won't be doing that. Not unless you want to go home with Mummy Dearest.'

Amber grimaced. 'Don't remind me.'

'I will, if you turn into one of those impossible patients who can never be pleased.'

'Are you talking from experience here?'

'I have to confess I was not the best patient in the world when my ankle was broken. I trust you will be much more…amenable. Now I really must go. I'll see you tomorrow.'

The moment Warwick disappeared from sight, Amber was besieged by doubts over her decision to accept his offer. What good could come of it? She wanted to get over the man, not fall even more in love with him. Which she might, if he showed her more of this noble side that he seemed to have suddenly acquired.

The only positive she could find about the prospect of living with Warwick as a friend rather than as a lover was maybe she would discover that, without the magic spell of his lovemaking, her so-called love for him would disappear like a puff of smoke. It was a vain hope but remotely possible. Sex had been a dominant part of their relationship up till now. It might have coloured her thinking. She'd read somewhere that it was common for young people to confuse lust and love. If that didn't prove to be the case, and she remained hopelessly in love with him, then maybe being with her without sleeping with her would make Warwick see that there was more to her than just being his penthouse pet. Maybe he would finally fall in love with *her*.

Wow! She hadn't thought of that.

For the first time since the accident Amber's spirits lifted.

'Now that's much better,' the ward nurse said when she came in to take Amber's blood pressure.

Amber blinked up at her. 'What do you mean?'

'You're almost smiling,' the woman replied. 'Must be because of that handsome fellow I saw by your bed just now. Is he your boyfriend?'

Amber almost told the truth, but decided a little white lie couldn't hurt. 'Yes,' she said. 'Yes, he is.'

'Lucky girl.'

'We've been living together for nearly a year,' Amber found herself adding.

'Even luckier.'

'He's English.'

The nurse laughed. 'He's a right hunk, that's what he is.'

'That too,' Amber agreed, smiling.

'I'd be hanging on to him, dear, if I were you.'

'I intend to,' Amber said, finally accepting it was worth the risk of more heartbreak to give her hopes and dreams of a future with Warwick one last chance.

But she had no idea, as she began actually looking forward to her convalescence, that there might be no hope of a future with Warwick Kincaid. No hope of anything but heartache and unhappiness…

CHAPTER ELEVEN

BY THE time Warwick let himself into his Point Piper apartment, he'd totally come to terms with his decision to look after Amber himself. There were no longer any doubts and definitely no recriminations. It was the right thing to do. The *only* thing to do, if he was going to live with himself after they parted.

Okay, so there were going to be some difficult moments. He hadn't gone six weeks without sex since he'd left boarding school at eighteen and entered Oxford University, not even when he'd broken his own ankle a few years back. There was nothing like physical inactivity and boredom to raise a man's testosterone levels. Within a couple of weeks of entering the rehabilitation clinic he'd been climbing the walls. Figuratively speaking, that was. He hadn't been climbing anything with that damned boot on. Fortunately, there'd been one very pretty nurse who hadn't minded going that extra mile for her patient, especially when that patient was presentable and single and very, very rich.

So, yes, Warwick wasn't in the habit of doing without.

But he was sure he could manage. How hard could it be?

Very hard, he accepted when he started packing

Amber's things. Damn, but her nightwear was sexy: no flannelette nighties for her. Everything was made of satin, silk and lace, something he should have realised since he'd bought most of the garments for her. Of course, he always kept the temperature in this apartment at a very pleasant level. Even in the winter, Amber had been able to swan around in flimsy lingerie without fear of catching a chill.

And he'd liked her swanning around in flimsy lingerie.

Bad train of thought, Warwick. Very bad train of thought!

Grimacing, he pushed the lingerie drawer firmly shut before emptying her underwear drawer into a bag without further inspection, knowing it would be just as sexy. After that he proceeded into the bathroom where he scooped all of her skin and hair care products into a large toilet bag, grabbed her bathrobe off the back of the door, then went back out into the bedroom where he stood, glaring at the bottles of perfumes sitting on her dressing table. They were all extremely expensive, exotic scents that he'd personally chosen for her and which turned him on.

'She never said anything about bringing her perfume,' he muttered. So he left them there, the same way he'd left the sexy lingerie behind. Tomorrow he'd go buy her some more modest nighties, which wouldn't make him wish he'd never suggested this crazy idea in the first place.

Her casual clothes didn't present any visual stimulation problems. But Warwick quickly realised that all Amber's skinny jeans were unlikely to fit over the rather bulky boot she'd have to wear to support her broken ankle. He recalled how he'd lived in roomy tracksuits during his recovery, ones where the pants had elastic around the ankles or zippers up the sides.

Amber didn't have any tracksuits. She didn't like them. She wore shorts or leggings to the gym.

He still threw all her jeans in with her other casual clothes, but he put a couple of pairs of jogging bottoms on his mental shopping list. Warwick recalled passing a large shopping centre between Gosford and Wamberal, which should have anything he needed to buy.

When he'd finally finished packing Amber's things, he filled a suitcase with some clothes for himself, after which he took a long hot shower and tried not to worry about how he would cope, living the life of a monk. By the time he climbed into bed, he was so darned tired that his mind shut down immediately.

His dreams, however, were not quite so kind. Like most dreams they were rather jumbled, but still vivid and unfortunately very erotic, and about Amber. In the dream just before he woke, she was lying naked in her aunt Kate's bed. He was standing by the bed, staring down at her, dying to climb in with her, but he couldn't seem to move. Then another man came into the room: it was Hansen. Warwick recognised the smarmy smile on his face. When Amber lifted the bedspread to invite him in with her, Warwick went to cry out. But no sound came out of his mouth, even though he was screaming in his head. When Hansen started kissing Amber, he shot awake and upright, his hands balled into tight fists by his side.

The realisation that it was only a dream brought some relief. But only to his mind, not his body. Warwick sighed, then climbed out of bed and headed for a decidedly cold shower, after which he returned to bed and just lay there, thinking about Amber and all that she'd said to him the previous day.

Despite being a man of considerable intelligence, Warwick wasn't used to deep and meaningful thinking. He'd given it up soon after he'd found out what the future held for him, making a conscious decision to live his life in the here and now, seeking pleasure and satisfaction in whatever took his fancy for as long as it lasted. He didn't let himself worry about what other people thought or felt. He didn't worry about outcomes, even with his many and varied investments.

Knowing what awaited him had been strangely liberating in that regard. What did it matter if he lost all his money, when compared with the inevitability of losing his mind?

Perversely, his disregard of risk had made him an even wealthier man than he'd been when his father died. He'd plunged into deals that a more careful man would not have considered, most of which had returned a profit. On the other hand, he'd never been greedy, taking his money out of the stock market when it had still been on the rise, just before the disastrous crash in 2001. Not because he'd foreseen the future. Warwick didn't think about the future. He just knew he'd already made good money and enough was enough.

People often said he was lucky. That always made him laugh. Lucky, he wasn't. But as the saying went, fortune did seem to favour the brave. Not that he would call himself brave, either. He was impulsive and reckless and, at times, downright foolish. On the other hand, however, he did have a good brain—a brilliant brain, one of his teachers had once said.

One day, however, that so-called brilliant brain would begin to stop functioning. When this would happen,

Warwick could not be absolutely sure. But given his family history, it seemed likely that the age of fifty would be his deadline.

So what are you planning to do for the next ten years, Warwick, my man? he asked himself as he lay there in the darkness, waiting for the dawn. More of the same? Or something different. Something a little more... worthy.

'An odd word, that,' Warwick muttered to himself. 'Worthy.'

What did it mean?

Suspecting that sleep was not likely to claim him now, Warwick climbed out of bed and padded, naked, out to the kitchen, where he set about making himself some coffee. The clock on the wall said it was ten past six. Soon the dark of night would lift and the sun would slide up over the horizon, heralding another day.

'What does it mean to live a worthy life?' he asked himself aloud as he waited for the electric jug to boil.

Warwick frowned. A year ago, he would never have been having this conversation with himself. He certainly wouldn't have been questioning his lifestyle or searching his soul for enlightenment over how to live what was left of his life.

But then, a year ago, he hadn't met Amber.

A year ago, he hadn't been loved.

Warwick didn't want Amber to ever look at him the way she'd looked at him yesterday. He wanted to see, if not love in her eyes, then at least admiration. He wanted her to be proud of him.

Which she might be, if he looked after her the way he'd vowed to last night. With his own two hands— those same two hands that had to be kept firmly off her delectable and highly desirable body.

Warwick's mouth twisted to one side as he envisaged all the intimate things he might have to do for her: help her dress and undress; help her in the bathroom; help her into bed. The list contained nothing but endless torment.

He had to be the worst masochist in the world to suggest it. Or a saint.

Unfortunately, he was neither. The next six weeks, he realised, were going to be sheer, unadulterated hell!

Shaking his head, Warwick took his coffee into the living room, where he settled down on the sofa that faced the water. There he sat, slowly sipping the steaming liquid whilst watching the dawn, at the same time making a mental list of all the things he had to do that day.

Inform the cleaning service that he was going away for six weeks. Visit the club and tell the construction manager that he would be liaising with him by phone and email for a while. Ring the hospital to see how the op went. Drive up to Gosford. Buy flowers. Visit Amber. Then go to that shopping centre.

There were several items in the B & B that would have to be replaced. That crocheted bedspread for one. No way was that staying! He'd buy a new quilt for the upstairs bedroom as well, the one he'd liked the most and in which he'd be sleeping. Because of course he wouldn't be sleeping in the same room as Amber.

Then there was the question of some air conditioning in the old lady's bedroom. And a new TV for Amber to watch. The ancient one in the corner didn't shout digital to him.

It was a lot to do in one day, but Warwick had no doubt he'd manage. It was amazing just how cooperative sales people could be when you threw in a cash bonus. He was determined that by the time Amber arrived home tomorrow everything would be ready for her!

CHAPTER TWELVE

An excerpt from Amber's new diary, written two weeks after her discharge from hospital:

Another long, wretchedly frustrating day! I can't stand not being able to get around without wearing that damned boot and pushing that hideous walking frame. Although it's the Rolls Royce of walking frames. Trust Warwick to only hire the very best. It even has a tray top and a basket underneath that I can carry things in, like books and stuff. But I can't seem to read. I used to like reading but not during the past two weeks. Warwick bought me a fancy iPod and downloaded lots of games on it, which was thoughtful of him, I suppose. But not what I wanted when I complained I was bored. The truth is I wanted Warwick to play games with me, not leave me alone to amuse myself. I'm sick of watching television, even if it is the latest flat-screen model which must have cost Warwick a tidy sum. When I first came home and saw all the things he'd bought—including an air conditioner for my bedroom—I told him that he shouldn't have. But he took no notice and hasn't stopped buying me things. I've given up objecting.

One thing I did do for myself was ring an agency and hire a woman to come in and help me shower and dress every morning. I knew I wouldn't be able to stand Warwick doing that for me. And he probably would have. He's been quite amazing, really. He's taught himself how to cook by following Aunt Kate's handwritten recipe books. Not that he doesn't occasionally order takeaway. We've had the odd Chinese and a pizza or two. Washing clothes hasn't presented any problem for him, either. Still, Aunt Kate installed a well-equipped laundry, including a tumble-dryer, with a list of simple instructions for guests taped to the wall near them. I know I shouldn't complain. He's doing everything he said he would. But I hate it. I hate his treating me like a flatmate he's mildly fond of. I hate it that he talks to Max more than he talks to me. But most of all I hate sleeping alone. Not that it bothers Warwick. It didn't even bother him when he came into my room last week and caught me sitting up in bed with nothing on. I was changing nighties at the time. But he didn't turn a hair. Didn't even really look. Which irritated me to death. He used to say I had the most beautiful breasts in the world. Suddenly, they don't even rate a second glance. So yes, maybe my frustration is sexual. Who knows? Have to go now, Diary. Warwick's at the door. You'll hear from me later.

WARWICK ALWAYS tapped on the door nowadays before entering Amber's bedroom, ever since he'd walked in one day last week and caught her in the act of changing her nightie. Seeing her sitting up in bed, naked from the waist up, was not helpful with his resolve to keep his hands off. He'd spent the rest of the day feeling frustration, which had only eased after he'd gone swimming in the sea, in a freezing cold surf.

When he came into the room this time, she was sitting in the armchair that faced the television, fully dressed in a velour maroon tracksuit, her long blonde hair twisted into a knot on top of her head. Despite not wearing make-up, she looked utterly beautiful but decidedly unhappy. Warwick wondered what she'd been writing in the diary that she'd asked him to buy for her the day after she'd left hospital and which was presently resting on her lap. A pen was still in her right hand.

'Dinner's ready,' he announced. 'Do you need any help getting out of that chair?'

Amber sighed as she put both the diary and pen down on the small side table. 'No, thanks. I'll be along shortly.'

Warwick's teeth clenched down hard in his jaw. He could understand her wanting to be independent. But he hated seeing her struggle to do things. Hated not being able to do what he thought was natural for a man to do for his woman.

'Damn it all,' he suddenly muttered and strode over to the chair, where he swept her up into his arms. 'Yes, yes, I know I'm supposed to keep my wicked hands off,' he growled as he carried her from the room. 'But there's a limit to any man's patience.'

She hooked her arms around his neck and stared up at him with her big lustrous blue eyes.

'I...I thought you didn't want me any more,' she choked out.

He ground to a halt in the hallway. 'I'm not carrying

you off to my bed, Amber,' he informed her brusquely. 'Just to the kitchen table for dinner.'

'Oh.' She flushed a dark red and dropped her eyes from his.

'Do you *want* me to take you up to my bed?'

Her eyes lifted back to his, their expression confused and uncertain. 'I don't know.'

She didn't know. Hell on earth, but she'd try the patience of a saint!

'Then let me do my best to make up your mind for you. If you say yes, then I'll quite happily make love to you. All night long if you wish. It hasn't been easy for me being here with you like this. Celibacy does not come naturally to me. But let me warn you, Amber, I will still leave when you're better. It won't change anything. Do not think that sleeping with me will make me stay, because it won't!'

Amber wished he hadn't added that last bit. Wished he'd stopped at how glad he would be to make love to her all night. Then she could have surrendered to the wild, rapturous heat that was racing through her veins and not worried about the future. She could have tried living the way he'd always lived: for the pleasure of the moment.

But, no, he had to tell the cold, hard facts, didn't he? Had to make her face the reality of his offer. Had to put the ball squarely back in her court.

Dear God, but he was cruel!

'In that case, take me to the kitchen,' she said with stiff pride.

'Fine,' Warwick bit out and did just that, depositing her in one of the kitchen chairs before swinging away to see to the food, grateful for the opportunity to collect himself.

For a split second there, he'd almost ignored her not very convincing 'no' and carried her upstairs to bed. Because he'd seen the truth in her eyes. Seen the yearning. She wanted him to make love to her, no doubt about that.

And damn it all, he wanted to make love to her!

But he hadn't come this far to fall at the first hurdle. He had to stay strong. Because it was obvious that Amber couldn't. The accident had made her vulnerable and weak. He would have no trouble seducing her, no trouble at all.

But seduction was not on the menu for tonight. Or any other night.

'I've cooked your aunt's recipe for Hungarian goulash,' he said as he returned to the table with their meals. 'Right down to the dash of Worcestershire sauce. But I didn't cook potatoes with it, just rice.'

'It looks very nice,' Amber said rather dully as she picked up her fork.

'Do you want a glass of red with it?' he asked as he picked up the bottle he'd bought earlier and placed on the table along with two of her aunt's very elegant wine glasses. 'I know you're not mad about red but you can't really drink white with this. And the Merlot is particularly good. Very soft on the palate.'

'Whatever,' she said with an indifferent shrug.

Warwick quickly saw that dinner was going to be a sombre affair. And he was right: Amber didn't speak, just forked the goulash into her mouth like an automaton. She ate it all, though, which was some consolation for the effort it had taken to make the darned food. He'd been in the kitchen for hours. Not that he really minded. Strangely enough, Warwick had found that he quite enjoyed cooking, even if he did take ages to do everything.

But he hated the cleaning up afterwards. Actually, he hated cleaning in general. To put it bluntly, cleaning sucked. He would have hired a housekeeper if he hadn't needed as many activities as possible to distract and tire him, firmly believing the adage about the devil and idle hands. So, along with the housework and the shopping, he ran along the beach twice a day, in the morning by himself and every afternoon with Max, who seemed to have warmed to him at last. Max had actually come to the house last evening after dinner with a bottle of port and they'd drunk it together whilst they chatted away about business, mostly the hotel industry.

They didn't touch upon personal affairs, for which Warwick was grateful. It would have been awkward to explain about his situation where Amber was concerned without coming out looking the baddie. Which he was, of course. But he liked Max and didn't want the man to begin thinking badly of him again. So when Max invited them both to a barbecue at his house this coming weekend, as one would any normal couple, he'd said yes.

But he hadn't told Amber yet, something he would have to remedy since Tara occasionally dropped in to see Amber and would probably mention the invitation herself.

'By the way,' he said as soon as Amber put her fork down. 'Max and Tara have invited us to a barbecue at their place this Saturday. Not in the evening. At lunchtime.'

'Oh?' she said archly. 'And when did this happen?'

'Last night.'

'Really. And what did you say?'

'I said yes.'

'Without asking me first.'

'Yes.'

Amber tried not to explode. But really, he was incorrigible.

'I don't want to go,' she lied. In truth, she was dying to get out of this house for a while.

'If you don't, I'll have to tell them the truth.'

'Then tell them the truth!'

'To what end? They'll feel uncomfortable and so will we.'

'*You're* the one who'll feel uncomfortable,' Amber snapped.

'True. But I'm thinking of you as well. Max and Tara are good people. Good friends. You'll need them after I leave. Why jeopardise their friendship by airing all our dirty linen in front of them at this stage? Far better that we go on pretending that we are what they think we are: lovers. That way, when I finally leave, they're sure to rally around you and give you all the support you need.'

'So this has nothing to do with your new best mate realising that Aunt Kate was right about you being a cold-blooded bastard?'

Warwick had to smile. Amber was one smart cookie. But then, he'd always thought that. She was the one who underestimated herself.

'That could also be a factor,' he admitted, and refilled his wine glass.

'A very big factor. Oh, all right. We'll go to the stupid barbecue, then. Though goodness knows what I'm going to wear.'

'You have four days before the weekend. We'll sort something out. Now, are you going to drink some more of this wine or not?'

'No. I don't much like it.'

'Fine,' he said with a slightly weary sigh. 'I'll carry you back to your room, then.'

'No, you won't. I'll make my own way back.'

His face reflected his exasperation. 'And how, pray tell, are you going to do that? The walking frame's still in the bedroom.'

'I'm sure you wouldn't mind getting it for me.'

'Then you'd be wrong,' he said sharply, and lifted his wine glass to his lips. Damn the girl, but he was not some lackey to be ordered around without any manners.

'*Please*, Warwick,' she said.

'You haven't thanked me for dinner.'

Amber rolled her eyes. 'Thank you for dinner.'

'Fine,' he said, and put down his glass. '*Now* I'll go get the walking frame.'

As Amber watched him stand up and walk from the room she could not help noticing how well Warwick was looking. His face was nicely tanned from all the running he'd been doing and his body looked extra hard and lean, especially his butt. Not that she needed any imagination to envisage what lay beneath the tight-fitting jeans he was wearing. She knew every inch of Warwick's body, and she loved every single part of it.

But it was what he did with that body that she loved the most. His lovemaking technique was superb. Amber had had limited lovers in her life. But she felt sure she could have had a hundred sexual partners and none of them would have compared with Warwick.

By the time he re-entered the kitchen with the walking frame Amber found herself staring at him shamelessly. Thankfully, Warwick's eyes were firmly on the floor and did not witness her shocking lack of decorum, not to mention common sense. Hadn't she learnt her lesson earlier on? She'd been so close to giving in and saying, yes, please, shag me all night and we won't worry about tomorrow! Which was insane, since she wasn't on the pill any more. She'd stopped taking it on the day of the accident, thinking it was a total waste of time.

To climb back into bed with Warwick would have been silly enough. To risk an unwanted pregnancy was beyond the pale. And she might have done just that, because once back in his arms she'd have been so turned on that she would not have wanted to stop proceedings by mentioning her lack of protection.

Heaven help her, but she was a fool!

A severely self-chastened Amber had cooled her lust-filled eyes by the time Warwick glanced up.

'Thank you again,' she said a bit stiffly.

'My pleasure,' he returned in that wonderfully polite and cultured British accent of his. 'I'll leave you to it, then, shall I?'

'Yes, please.'

'In that case I might take myself out for a walk. Try not to fall over whilst I'm gone, will you?'

Their eyes clashed. His were wryly amused, hers, instantly rebellious.

Amber tried to think of something witty to shoot back at him. But before anything came to her mind, Warwick had whirled on his heels and left the room.

'Damn it!' she muttered, hating it that he had had the last word.

His banging the back door shut with a degree of venom showed her, however, that he was not as coolly composed as he liked to pretend. She went to bed, pleased by the notion that Warwick was as frustrated as she was.

Sleep would not come, however, her mind as agitated as her body.

It had been a mistake, she finally accepted, having Warwick look after her. She should have gone home to her mother. She could still do that, she supposed. Her mother was in regular contact, ringing her at least every second day. Though she hadn't been up to visit her daughter as yet. She claimed she'd caught the flu the day after Amber's accident and hadn't felt up to the drive.

Amber wasn't entirely convinced of this. Doreen didn't sound all that sick. But perhaps she was being paranoid.

Even so it was enough to make Amber reluctant to ask her mother for help. Under the circumstances, there was no alternative but to see this nightmare through.

Three and a half more weeks she had to endure. What a ghastly thought!

CHAPTER THIRTEEN

Four days later, Amber woke, feeling marginally better at the prospect of actually going out that day, dressed in something really nice for a change. Tara had been kind enough to go shopping for her, bringing back several outfits from a local boutique for Amber to have a look at.

One had stood out as both practical and beautiful, a pale blue woollen trouser suit with flared trousers that totally hid the ugly boot she had to wear. It had a long cardigan-style jacket, which was both stylish and contemporary, and a cream silk cami to wear underneath.

Amber had known without trying it on that it would be perfect.

The only trouble was getting it on. Judy was away for the weekend and couldn't come in to shower and dress her as usual.

'I think you can manage on your own now,' Judy had said the day before. 'Or you can get Warwick to help you.'

Amber had agreed to the woman's face, but privately resolved that she would manage on her own, even if it killed her.

Admittedly, she was much steadier on her feet these days. It was three weeks now since her fall, the wound from the operation had healed and the stitches were out. But it was still painful to put her weight on her ankle without the boot. She could manage to take herself to the bathroom easily, though she couldn't leave the boot on in the shower as it would get very wet indeed. There was a stool in the corner for her to sit on, but Amber doubted she could get in and out of the shower stall without help. Which meant she would have to ask Warwick.

Not a good idea!

In the end she managed by wrapping the whole boot in cling-wrap. But it took her ages. Drying herself afterwards was particularly awkward, since she had to hold on to the towel rail whilst wiping herself down single-handed. Drying her hair wouldn't be so bad as she'd thought ahead and set up her dryer on the bed, along with her underwear.

Possibly it was the noise of the hair-dryer that masked Warwick's knock on the door. Whatever, suddenly, without warning, the door opened and he strode in, grinding to a abrupt halt when he saw that Amber was sitting on the side of the bed, stark naked.

'Oh!' she gasped, and snatched up a pillow to hold in front of her.

He laughed. 'A bit late for that, don't you think? I did knock. Obviously you didn't hear me. I just wanted to see how you were getting on. It's a quarter to twelve. I said we'd be there around twelve.'

Amber pulled a face. 'I'm sorry but I won't be ready for at least another fifteen minutes. I haven't any make-up on and I'm not dressed yet.'

'Um, yes, I did see that,' he said.

Warwick could not believe it when she blushed. How many times had he seen her naked?

So why, Warwick, old man, did the sight of her sitting sweetly like that turn you on instantly?

'It took me for ever in the shower,' she said, clearly flustered by his presence.

Maybe she could see that he was excited. His jeans were fairly fitted.

'I'll give Max a call and tell him we'll be fifteen minutes late,' Warwick said, turning to walk quickly from the room. No point in embarrassing both of them further. Or in wanting what he could no longer have.

Fifteen minutes later he knocked on the bedroom door again.

'Yes, you can come in,' Amber replied. 'I'm ready.'

Warwick did his best not to let the sight of her affect him this time, but she looked achingly beautiful.

'You look lovely,' he said. 'Blue suits you.'

'Thank you. You look very nice too.'

'Nice?' he repeated drily. 'I'll have you know I spent a small fortune on this outfit!' A total lie. The black jeans and black and grey striped shirt had cost him around two hundred dollars in a menswear shop at Erina Fair, and the black leather jacket had been on sale for two-fifty at the same place.

He'd seen the complete outfit in the window, liked it, walked in and bought the lot, a most unusual thing for him to do. A few weeks ago he would never have purchased ready-to-wear clothes. He'd always had everything tailor-made. But since coming to Wamberal he no longer cared about such things. They seemed… unimportant.

Neither did he care about arriving at Max's in Aunt Kate's car rather than his made-to-impress Ferrari. All he cared about was Amber's comfort.

'I've never actually been here before,' Amber said

when they arrived at Max's address, which was less than a kilometre away from the B & B. Even from the street, it looked impressive: a multi-level cement-rendered house right on the beach. But what else would one expect? Max was a seriously wealthy man.

Amber and Warwick were stopped in front of the high-security gates for little more than ten seconds before they slid open to reveal an enclosed courtyard graced by tall palm trees and a fountain in the middle. Warwick drove in and followed the paved circular drive, bypassing a large garage complex on their left before pulling up in front of an elegantly columned portico. One of the two massive wooden front doors opened as soon as he turned off the engine, Max emerging with a welcoming smile on his face.

The two men helped Amber out of the car, Amber having refused to bring the walking frame along.

'You're just in time,' Max said to them both as they made their way slowly up the steps. 'I opened a bottle of simply marvellous red ten minutes ago and it should be ready to drink by now. But you don't have to worry, Amber. Warwick told me you're not a red girl, so I've put a couple of bottles of Sauvignon Blanc on ice for you.'

'A couple of bottles!' she exclaimed. 'I'll be under the table before I'm finished.'

'I wouldn't think so. Tara prefers white as well. She'll help you drink it. This way…'

'What a lovely home you have,' Amber said as she was led through the spacious foyer into the body of the house.

She'd been expecting something way different from the décor that greeted her. In the time she'd spent with Warwick in Sydney, she'd gone to a lot of dinner parties in the homes of the rich and famous. Amber had found that she could divide the décor of these houses into two types: those that were filled to the rafters with chandeliers, antiques and more marble than the Vatican; and then there were the ones whose owners invariably had a penchant for black and white, plus the kind of stylistic minimalist furniture that looked good in a photospread but lacked both warmth and comfort in reality.

Tara and Max's home was filled with both warmth *and* comfort, without an antique or a chandelier in sight. The main living area was open-plan, with recessed lighting and polished wooden floors covered by lush cream rugs, the same colours as the walls.

Everything was modern, yet casual: the soft-looking leather lounge suite in a lovely buttery yellow; the kitchen with its cream cupboards and stone bench tops. There was a play area for the children to one side, an informal eating area on the other, and a huge flat-screen television built into the back wall, on either side of which were floor-to-ceiling glass doors, beyond which Amber glimpsed a decked terrace and a pool.

'Tara's just getting Jasmine dressed after her morning nap,' Max said, explaining his wife's absence. 'But she won't be long.'

'That's all right,' Amber replied. 'Take me out to that table on the terrace and I'll just sit in the sunshine.'

'Good idea. I'll pour you some wine in a jiffy but first I want Warwick to come and meet Stevie. He's outside playing in the sandpit as usual.'

Warwick had forgotten about Max's children when he'd accepted the invitation to this barbecue. He wasn't good with kids, perhaps because he knew he would never have any. He was often impatient with them, and indifferent to the many qualities their parents proudly pointed out.

But it was impossible not to like Stevie. Not only was he a good-looking child, he was totally lacking in that annoying energy that small children seemed incapable of harnessing. He also didn't seem to need to be constantly entertained, being perfectly happy playing in the sandpit by himself, making roads and garages for his toy cars.

'What a great boy you have there,' Warwick said as the two men returned to the house.

'We think so. He's nothing like I was as a child,' Max said as he went about getting everyone a drink. 'I was a right little pain in the butt. Always wanting attention, always wanting to be first. Stevie's extremely self-contained and very easy-going. He takes after my kid brother, who had the most wonderfully placid nature. His name was Stevie, too. Unfortunately he died young, of testicular cancer.'

'What rotten luck.'

'I don't think it was totally a question of luck. Mum said he probably inherited the gene which caused it.'

Any talk of inheriting bad genes always got Warwick's attention. 'Aren't you worried you might have inherited it as well?'

'Nope. Stevie and I have different dads. Stevie's father died young of cancer. My dad's still going strong. He did have a stroke a few years back, but he's recovered well.'

'Your mother married twice, did she?'

When Max hesitated to answer Warwick knew he'd possibly touched a nerve.

'No,' Max said eventually. 'Mum had an affair.'

'Ah…'

Max shrugged. 'It wasn't entirely her fault. My dad was away from home a lot. I guess she was lonely.'

'Does your father know about your mother's affair, and your brother's paternity?'

'He didn't at first. When he found out, he did what most men do when faced with something unthinkable. He ran away. Well, not literally. But he travelled even more than he already did.'

Which is what I do, Warwick conceded. Travel a lot. Go from place to place, business to business, woman to woman.

And it had worked well for him up till now. He hadn't allowed himself time to think. Thinking inevitably led to depression and other more terrible thoughts. He felt genuinely sorry for Max's father and understood fully his methods of dealing with his wife's infidelity.

'It must have been a very difficult time for him,' he said sincerely.

'It was a very difficult time for me, too,' Max said a bit sharply. But then he shrugged. 'But that's all past. No point in living in the past.'

'No point at all,' Warwick agreed. It was the future that was the worry.

'Here. Take this glass of white out to your girl. I'll go see what's keeping Tara.'

Warwick stood for a long moment after Max disappeared. Finally he gave himself a mental shake and headed for the terrace.

'It *is* good to get out of that bedroom for a while,' Amber said as he handed her the glass of white.

'Max has gone to see what's keeping Tara,' he told her, and took a sip of his own wine. 'Mmm. This is a *very* good red.'

'Oh, you men and red wine,' Amber said somewhat

impatiently. 'I don't know what you see in it. Give me white any day.'

'You'll change your mind when your taste buds mature. Ah, here's Tara now. With little Jasmine, isn't it?'

How strange, Warwick thought as he looked Max's wife up and down. She was a really stunning-looking blonde, and had a great figure, shown to advantage in tight white jeans and an emerald green mohair jumper that matched her green eyes.

But she didn't make his heart race the way Amber could, which perhaps was just as well.

Warwick soon saw that Max's three-year-old daughter was absolutely nothing like her older brother, either in looks or in nature. Whilst Stevie was an attractive enough child, Jasmine promised to be a great beauty, with her mother's heart-shaped face, soft blonde hair and striking green eyes. On top of that, where Stevie didn't like attention, Jasmine lapped it up. She quickly demanded that 'Uncle Wawie' pick her up and hold her whilst her daddy attended to the barbecue.

Amber had already gone back inside with Tara so Warwick could find no reason to refuse.

'Jasmine loves to watch me do the barbecue, don't you, princess?' Max said indulgently after Warwick had hoisted Jasmine up high into his arms.

'Daddy sometimes burns the meat,' his daughter said, somewhat precociously for a three-year-old. ''Specially the sausages. That's why I have to watch. You can watch too, Uncle Wawie.'

Max rolled his eyes. 'What say Uncle Wawie looks after the sausages whilst I do the steak?'

Jasmine pouted her already pouty lips. 'He can't do

that, Daddy. He only has two hands and they're both busy.'

'Yes, Max,' Warwick said. 'Very busy.' And he picked up his wine glass with his free hand and took an appreciative swallow.

Max shot him a droll look. 'I tell you what, Jasmine. Why don't you go over and play with Stevie in the sandpit? He must be lonely there all alone.'

'Stevie likes playing 'lone, Daddy. I want to stay here.' And she batted her eyelashes shamelessly at Warwick.

Suddenly, it killed him, the fact that he would never have a gorgeous little girl of his own like this. Or a great son like Stevie.

If only he hadn't been his father's son, he could have married Amber, and had a family like Max's. He could have lived up here in a house just like this. Could have grown old with Amber the way Max would probably grow old with Tara. Could have become a grandfather, even.

But that would never be.

Max was so right. It was all a matter of inheritance.

Warwick knew then that he could not bear to stay with Amber much longer. He had to go back to the life he'd had before, where nothing and no one mattered to him. This was much too painful.

Maybe he'd be able to last another three weeks, but he seriously doubted it.

'Is anything wrong, Warwick?'

Max's query snapped him out of his increasingly dark thoughts. 'No. Why?'

'You were looking a bit bleak there.'

'What does bleak mean, Daddy?' Jasmine asked.

'It means sad.'

'Are you sad, Uncle Wawie?'

'I think I just need to eat,' Warwick said by way of an excuse. 'This is great wine but it packs a powerful punch.'

'Well, the meat's just about done. And not at all burnt, missie,' Max added, giving his little girl a narrowed-eyed glare.

She just giggled.

'Tara!' he called out. 'How's that salad coming along?'

'Everything's on the table, waiting for you,' she called back.

'In that case, the meat is on its way. And so are we! Stevie, go wash your hands. Lunch is ready.'

CHAPTER FOURTEEN

'It's been a lovely day,' Amber said to Tara shortly after four-thirty. They were alone in the kitchen, the men having taken the children for a walk along the beach. 'Thank you so much for inviting us.'

Tara straightened up from where she'd been stacking the dishwasher. 'Thank *you* for coming,' she said. 'It's not often we entertain these days. Other than family, that is. Children have a way of putting a stop to your social life. Not that I mind. I like being a homebody.'

'And Max?' Amber asked. 'Does he mind?'

Tara smiled a soft smile. 'I used to worry that he'd miss the jet-setting lifestyle he had before we got married. But he doesn't. Of course we do still travel quite a bit. But it's always as a family. Max never goes alone any more.'

'You both do seem very happy.'

'We are. And you, Amber? Are you happy with Warwick?'

Amber almost confided in her. But only almost.

'Very,' she said, and forced a smile to her mouth.

'Do you think you might get married at some stage?'

Amber decided not to carry her lies too far. 'Warwick's not keen on marriage.'

'Um. Yes, so I heard.'

'From whom?'

'Kate.'

'What did she say, exactly?'

Tara pulled a face. 'I don't think I can repeat it.'

'As bad as that, eh?'

'Look, men can change,' Tara said kindly. 'When I first met Max, he told me marriage wasn't on his agenda. At the time, he was in charge of over a dozen international hotels and spent half his life on planes.'

'So what changed him? From what I can see he's the perfect family man.'

Tara's laugh was soft and melodic. 'Having little Stevie changed him.'

Amber's heart sank. 'Unfortunately, Warwick doesn't want children any more than he wants marriage.'

'A lot of men say that, till they have them. Max said he didn't want children either, but when I fell pregnant he soon changed his mind and asked me to marry him.'

'That's because he loves you.'

Tara frowned at Amber. 'You don't think Warwick loves you?'

Amber bit her bottom lip. Now she'd done it. 'Well, I…er…he's never said that he does.'

'That doesn't mean anything much with men like Warwick. I can see what type he is.'

'What type is that?'

'Reserved and a bit uptight. You know, typically British.'

Amber had to laugh. 'Warwick's not at all like that. He's the most impulsive, reckless, crazy man I've ever met.'

'Really?'

'Yes, really!'

'Heavens, I would never have guessed. He seems so... conservative. How is he in bed? Or shouldn't I ask?'

Amber flushed. 'I have no complaints.'

Tara laughed. 'Now who's being reserved and up-tight?'

Amber laughed as well.

'Man, but it's getting nippy out there!'

Amber swung slowly round on the kitchen stool at the sound of Max's voice. He was standing on the mat just inside the sliding glass door, wiping his feet and rubbing his hands vigorously together. Warwick was still outside on the terrace, Amber saw, brushing the sand down from Jasmine's clothes. When Stevie followed his father inside, Max took his son's hand and led the boy over to his mother.

'You should have seen the sandcastle Warwick and Stevie built together,' Max told Tara. 'It even had a moat.'

'I used a cuttlefish bone I found as a drawbridge,' Stevie added proudly.

'What a clever boy you are,' Tara said.

Stevie beamed with pleasure at his mother's compliment. 'Uncle Warwick said he'd help me build another one soon.'

'That's kind of him,' Tara replied. 'But not right now. Now, it's bath time.'

'And time we went home,' Warwick said as he came inside, carrying Jasmine.

'I don't want Uncle Wawie to go home,' Jasmine said with her by-now-familiar pout.

'I don't want to either, sweetie,' he said. 'But Aunty Amber has a broken ankle and gets tired easily. I should take her home and put her to bed.'

'She has to have a bath first,' Jasmine pointed out.

'She had a shower this morning.'

'Mummy won't let us have showers,' Jasmine said. 'Not till we're older.'

'Baths are much better,' Stevie piped up. 'You can play in the bath.'

'Here, I'll take Jasmine,' Tara said, and took Jasmine out of Warwick's arms. 'Max, you give Warwick a hand with getting Amber down those front steps, will you? Sorry to love you and leave you. But these two darlings are very much children of routine. Get out of it and it's bedlam.'

Was it fate that Max should accompany them outside?

Whatever, it was certainly Max who said the fatal words that put the idea into Amber's head.

'Thanks for your help with the kids, Warwick,' Max said as both men helped Amber down the steps. 'You were incredibly patient with Jasmine. You know, you'd make a great father.'

Warwick said something offhand in return but Amber didn't quite catch it. Her mind was already elsewhere.

Warwick *would* make a great father, she'd begun thinking. She too had noticed how good he was with Max's kids, especially Jasmine. His patience and gentleness had surprised her.

Okay, so he was wary of fatherhood. Probably because of his own neglectful father, plus the abandonment of his mother. He hadn't exactly had good examples of parenthood.

But basically he was an honorable man, despite the rather decadent life he'd chosen to live so far. A decent man: look how he'd stayed to look after her. *And* he'd kept his hands off as promised.

But he wouldn't, if she gave him the green light. He'd

pretty well admitted the other night that celibacy was proving difficult. A highly sexed man like Warwick wouldn't take much seducing, provided she could convince him that all she wanted from him was sex. That might be a bit tricky, but she'd think of something.

Of course, he had no idea she'd gone off the pill. She hadn't told him. There'd been no reason to. If they went to bed, he would not imagine for one moment that she'd be trying to conceive his child.

Heavens, just the thought of doing such a bold thing took her breath away!

'Something wrong?' Warwick asked.

'What?' Only then did Amber realise they were on the road driving home. She couldn't even remember saying goodbye to Max.

'You made a sort of gasping sound. Like you'd had a fright.'

'Oh, that,' she said. 'I moved my foot and it hurt.'

'You've done too much today,' he chided, though gently. 'You should have let me bring the walking frame.'

'Warwick, don't fuss. I'm fine. It was just a twinge.'

'It sounded like more than that.'

'I'll take some painkillers when I get home.'

How was she going to seduce the man when he thought she was in pain?

Yet she would have to seduce him if she wanted to have his baby. And she did—more than anything else in the world. So why shouldn't she try to make it happen? Why should she lose *everything*? And who knew? If she was successful, if falling pregnant became a reality, Warwick just might do a Max and change his mind about marriage and children. He might even realise he loved her after all.

There again, he might not. Which meant she would have to raise his child all by herself...

It was a possibility that had to be faced.

Her mother would be furious with her. But Aunt Kate would have understood. Amber knew all about the baby Aunt Kate had once conceived and which she'd terminated when the father of the child became abusive to her. Even so, the poor woman had always regretted what she'd done. She'd once told Amber that if *she* became pregnant when she was still single, she should keep her child, no matter what. Kate'd said she would help her if the father wouldn't.

Well, Aunt Kate had already helped her, hadn't she? She'd left Amber her lovely house and her car. And a legacy of self-esteem and independent thinking.

I can do this, Amber decided by the time they arrived back at the B & B. I *have* to do this. It's not wrong, it's right. For both of us.

CHAPTER FIFTEEN

WARWICK parked the Astra as close as possible to the back porch, unlocking and opening the back door of the house before returning to the car to help Amber out.

'If you don't object,' he said, 'it will be much quicker if I carry you inside.'

Surprise flickered in her big blue eyes. Surprise… and something else.

Damn, but he could usually read her like a book. This time, however, her thoughts remained hidden to him. She'd been very quiet since leaving Max's house. Clearly, her ankle was aching badly, which was another reason for him to carry her inside.

'I suppose it's all right,' she said with a resigned-sounding sigh.

'Trust me, I wouldn't do this if it wasn't necessary,' he ground out as he scooped her up into his arms.

Masochism had never been his style. Till these last three weeks, that was. Living with Amber on a platonic basis was masochism in the extreme. Holding her close like this was the icing on the cake of his self torture.

Warwick swallowed hard when her arms tightened around his neck, bringing his head forward slightly and pressing his nose and mouth against the fragrant soft-ness of her hair. She smelled wonderful, *felt* wonderful.

His own arms tightened around her, his resolve not to make love to her wavering in the face of emotions that carried even more temptation than the fact that he was fiercely frustrated.

It wasn't the need for sex that would be his downfall, Warwick realised as he carried her inside. There were other feelings—other needs—much more powerful, the main one being the need to see her eyes light up with desire for him one last time.

'Amber,' he said, grinding to a halt in the hallway outside her bedroom door.

Her eyes lifted to gaze up at him. 'What?'

'I'm sorry,' he said.

'Sorry for what?'

'For this…'

The moment his lips crashed down on hers, something happened inside Warwick, something he'd never experienced before. His heart felt as if it had exploded, a hot mushroom cloud of emotion bursting up through his chest and into his head, leaving him feeling dizzy and disorientated.

But as the kissing continued it wasn't long before Warwick's responses changed from the emotional to the physical. Desire kicked in, fierce and urgent, his tongue diving deep into her gasping mouth till he had to wrench his mouth away and drag in a badly needed lungful of air.

'Don't tell me to stop,' he bit out harshly.

She didn't say a single word. Maybe she couldn't. She looked stunned.

He didn't wait. He carried her up the stairs, taking them two at a time. Once in his bedroom he laid her down on the bed before gathering her back up into his arms and kissing her over and over till he was sure she wouldn't change her mind and say no.

Only then did Warwick start to undress her, confident enough by then to take his time. Which was what he'd always liked to do with her. Take his time.

Slowly, gently, he removed her cardigan, then the rest of her clothes till she lay there in nothing but her impossibly sexy underwear, and that most unattractive boot.

'You won't be needing this on for a while,' he said as he undid the straps, carefully easing the boot off her foot.

'Am I hurting you?' he asked, glancing up at her face.

'No,' she replied.

And in truth he couldn't see any pain in her eyes. Just the most beguiling excitement.

'Please don't talk,' she suddenly choked out.

Her request startled him, then worried him. Underneath her obvious excitement, was she upset over doing this?

Yes, of course she was, he accepted. But it was too late now, way too late.

Once the boot was removed, he took her hands and pulled her up into a sitting position so that he could undo her bra. Her shoulders stiffened once the fastener gave way, a shiver running down her spine as he slowly pushed the bra straps down her arms. He doubted it was a shiver from being chilled. He'd left the heating on all day, not wanting to return to a cold house.

No, it was a shiver of erotic anticipation.

Once the bra was dispensed with, he ran a fingertip up and down her spine, building on the delicious tension he could feel in her body. When a more fierce shudder ran through her he eased her back onto the bed, arranging pillows behind her head till she looked comfortable.

The temptation to play with her beautiful breasts was acute. But he didn't want to do that just yet, not whilst he was still dressed. He wanted to be ready when she was ready. Which he suspected would not be far off if he kept up the foreplay. Her eyes were clinging to his the way they often did when she was hopelessly turned on.

Leaving her panties in place—to have her lying before him totally nude at this stage would be a mistake—he set about slowly undressing himself, using the time away from touching her to regain some control over his own wildly clamouring flesh. Maybe her ankle wasn't giving her any pain, but some parts of *his* body certainly were. Women didn't realise just how uncomfortable some erections could be. The one he had at this moment was nothing short of cruel. It was to be hoped that it didn't look as angry as it felt. He didn't want to frighten her.

Amber could not believe how incredibly exciting it was, watching Warwick undress like this. He'd never done a slow strip for her before. It was a relief to be able to look at him openly and not feel guilty about it.

He was a hunk all right. That nurse had been so right about that. A gorgeous hunk, and all hers. At least for tonight. What tomorrow morning would bring Amber did not know. All she could be sure of was the here and now. And that promised the kind of pleasure that only Warwick could give her—the kind of pleasure that no girl could resist.

For a brief moment, whether she fell pregnant or not no longer seemed crucial: she wanted to be here with him no matter what.

When Warwick finally slipped off his underpants he saw her eyes widen a little but not with fear. Flattered by her reaction, he stretched out beside her on the bed and began caressing her nipples in the way he knew she loved him to, first with his fingers and then with his mouth. When her back started arching from the bed, he moved on, trailing his mouth down past her navel till he encountered the top edge of her satin panties.

She trembled uncontrollably when he ran a hand up her thigh and slipped it under the leg elastic.

She was wet down there, *very* wet.

Removing his hand, he then removed her panties, sliding them slowly down her legs, holding her dilated eyes with his at the same time. Once the panties were dispensed with, he eased her legs apart then bent them up at the knees. Carefully, so that he didn't bump into her damaged ankle, he settled himself between her thighs and slowly, very slowly, pushed himself into her.

It was then that it happened again, that overwhelming rush of emotion that flooded his body and tightened his chest till he thought he might be having a heart attack.

'Dear God,' he actually cried out.

'What is it?' she said immediately. 'What's wrong?'

Nothing was *wrong*, he finally realised as enlightenment hit.

For a long moment he just stared down at her, at her lovely face, her lovely body and her even more lovely soul.

So *this* was what falling in love felt like.

'Nothing's wrong,' he replied, his voice husky. 'You just take my breath away.'

The compliment brought tears to Amber's eyes, and hope to her heart.

'Don't you dare cry,' he said thickly.

She blinked madly. 'I won't. I promise.'

'Let's just enjoy each other tonight, the way we used to.'

'All right,' she agreed.

But down deep, in that place where guilt festered, Amber knew that tonight was different from what they used to do. Tonight she was deceiving Warwick, big time. Tonight she had a secret agenda.

And whilst she had no intention of telling Warwick the truth, it struck Amber that maybe her troubled conscience would stop her from enjoying the sex the way she used to. Perhaps she would have to fake an orgasm or two, something she'd never had to do with Warwick before.

It was a worrying and slightly depressing thought.

'Good girl,' he said, and began to move, using that tantalising but powerful rhythm where he would almost withdraw before plunging back into her like a sword filling its scabbard to the hilt.

Soon, all worry had ceased, all her thoughts focusing on the exquisite sensations he was evoking. She knew, well before it happened, that she would not have to fake her orgasm. How silly of her to imagine that could ever be the case!

Her hands gripped handfuls of the quilt, trying to hold on to the pleasure, trying to make it last.

A futile exercise!

She cried out as she came, her bottom lifting from the bed at the same moment that he reached release. He cried out too, as his seed shot, hot and strong, into her womb. Only then, as he shuddered into her, did she think of the child whom this mating might produce. Just the thought of it brought an elation—and an emotion—which was difficult to control. She wanted to laugh and to cry at the same time. It was the strangest feeling, both joyful and sad.

She turned her head away and closed her eyes tightly shut, afraid to look up at him, afraid of what he might see.

'I'm sorry, Amber,' he said, and stroked a gentle hand down her cheek. 'I know this was not what you wanted.'

She could not bear to let him think that. Could not *bear* it!

'Don't be silly!' she exclaimed, her eyelids flying upwards as her head turned to face him. 'It's exactly what I wanted. I haven't liked being celibate any more than you have.'

His eyebrows lifted at her words. 'Does that mean I'm not going to have my wrists slapped for seducing you?'

'For pity's sake, Warwick, you didn't seduce me. I'm as responsible for what happened just now as you were. I could have said no at some point but I didn't. I *chose* to let you make love to me.'

'And will you choose to let me make love to you some more?' he asked, a sudden movement of his hips reminding her that he was still deep inside her and not totally spent, by the feel of him.

A memory popped into her mind, of a television programme she'd once seen about fertility problems, where it had been explained that too much sex was not conducive to conception. It was more a matter of quality rather than quantity, and of timing.

The trouble was Amber wasn't quite sure when she might ovulate.

Was more than once a night too much? she wondered.

'I'll take your silence for a yes,' Warwick said, and started to move, rocking backwards and forwards in a slow, sensual rhythm.

Amber caught her bottom lip with her teeth in an effort not to moan. But it felt so delicious. *He* felt delicious.

She couldn't tell him to stop now. She just couldn't.

Tomorrow she'd be more in control.

Tomorrow she'd come up with a plan...

CHAPTER SIXTEEN

Excerpt from Amber's diary two weeks later.

Haven't been writing much in you lately. Guess I didn't really want to think too hard over what I've been doing. It's not in my nature to deceive anyone. I hate dishonesty. But really, what else can I do? I simply can't face the rest of my life living alone, like Aunt Kate did. I need a child to love. I need Warwick's child. It worries me though that we've been doing it too much—way, way too much. If that show I saw on television is right, then that's not the best way to conceive. And I'm running out of time. Warwick's still going to leave when the six weeks are up. He tells me so every now and then, usually after he's made mad passionate love to me, sweet sensitive man that he is. Not! Lord knows what I'm going to say to Mum and Dad when he goes. They came up to visit me last Sunday and you know what Warwick did? Cooked them a baked dinner. I tell you, they were dead impressed. Mum even admitted to me that she was wrong about him, that it was obvious he loved me and would marry me in the end. I have to confess she did put ideas into my head. So I asked

Warwick why he went to all that trouble, and do you know what he said? He said it was because he wanted my parents to see that he did care for me, and that I wasn't a total idiot to give up a year of my life to live with him. Which was not quite what I was hoping for, as you can imagine. I didn't cry, though. I haven't cried ever since Warwick said I was a cry baby, not even when my ankle hurt like hell. By the way, my foot's feeling great now. I've given up the walking frame and am just using a walking stick to get around. Warwick still carries me up and down the stairs, though, which I find very romantic. He helps me in the shower as well. Naturally, I told Judy she was no longer needed. Warwick's out shopping at the moment but he'll be back soon. I'm down in Aunt Kate's room whilst he's gone. Warwick says he'd worry about me if he left me upstairs. I think I just heard him drive in. Must go.

WARWICK CALLED out to Amber as he carried the first of the shopping bags inside. She didn't answer.

Frowning, he dumped the bags onto the kitchen table and walked across the hallway to the bedroom where he'd left her. She wasn't there. The bathroom door, however, was shut.

'Amber! Are you in there?' he called out from the doorway.

'Yes,' came a rather feeble reply through the bathroom door.

'Is everything all right?'

No answer this time.

Instant alarm had him striding over to the bathroom

door and knocking on it. 'Amber, what's going on in there?'

'Nothing,' she choked out.

He wasn't having any of that. But when he went to open the door he discovered that it was locked.

'If you don't tell me what's going on,' he ground out, 'I'm going to break this door down.'

He was about to do just that when the door opened and there stood a devastated-looking Amber, her lovely blue eyes awash with tears.

'Dear God, what is it? What's happened?'

'I can't tell you,' she cried.

'Why not?'

'I just can't!' she blurted out, then broke down entirely, almost falling over when her head dropped into her hands.

Warwick scooped her up into his arms and carried her over to the bed, where he laid her gently down on top of the quilt. There, she gave him one last traumatised look before she rolled over onto her side and curled up into the foetal position, her eyes squeezing shut as deep sobs racked her slender body.

'Go away!' she choked out when he bent to stroke her hair. 'Just go away!'

Warwick had never in his life felt so helpless, or so guilty. Because he didn't have to be told what was behind Amber's distress.

He was, somehow.

He didn't go away; he couldn't. He pulled up a chair by the bed and sat watching over her till her weeping subsided. Even so she didn't speak, just lay there staring blankly into space.

'It's me, isn't it?' he said bleakly at last. 'I've caused this.'

A deep sigh reverberated through her as she slowly straightened and looked up at him.

'I wish I could blame you but I can't,' she said in a dull, flat voice. 'It's all my own fault. I'm the one who did the wrong thing. And now I'm being punished.'

Warwick had no idea what she was talking about. 'What do you mean, punished? For what?'

Her eyes searched his face, her expression half guilty, half regretful.

'Shortly after I broke my ankle,' she said brokenly, 'I stopped taking the pill. No, please don't say anything. Let me finish first. Let me try to explain.'

Warwick's stomach had already fallen into a deep dark pit. For she didn't really have to explain. He knew why she hadn't told him she'd gone off the pill. And he knew exactly what had just happened.

Poor darling, he thought as a tidal wave of remorse washed through him, poor, poor darling.

'At first, I did it because I thought we were finished. Then I realised I wanted a baby,' she blurted out. 'No, that's not totally true. I wanted *your* baby. And I knew you'd never give me one willingly.' Her face twisted with raw emotion, her throat convulsing as she swallowed several times. 'Believe me when I tell you I wasn't trying to trap you into marriage or anything. I would never do that. I just wanted a small part of you to love after you left me. I knew all along it wasn't right. But you do dreadful things when you're desperate. Still, you don't have to worry,' she added, her voice turning bitter. 'As I'm sure you've gathered by now, I got my period just now. So I'm not pregnant. I'm sure you're relieved to hear that.'

Warwick sighed a deeply unhappy sigh. He'd been hoping to extricate himself from Amber's life without leaving behind too much hurt, and without revealing the wretched truth. But he could see now the extent of his delusion. He knew Amber loved him. How could he possibly think that staying all this time and making love to her as much as he had would not give her more pain?

'I'm not at all relieved, Amber,' he told her truthfully. 'I would dearly love you to have my child.'

She sat bolt upright in surprise, eyes blinking wide. 'You would?'

'Yes. But it's never going to be, my love.'

His *love*? Had she heard that right?

Amber frowned as she struggled to make sense of the rest of what he'd said. Was he sterile? Could that be the answer to his distancing himself from any form of commitment?

'What I'm about to tell you will come as a shock.'

Amber was all ears.

'You could not become pregnant by me because I have had a vasectomy…'

CHAPTER SEVENTEEN

'A VASECTOMY!' Amber exclaimed, her eyes rounding.
  'Yes.'

Warwick saw her shock turn to confusion.

'But why…why would you do something like that?'
she asked in disbelieving tones. 'And when? When did
you do it?'

Warwick sighed. 'I had it when I was twenty.'

Amber's mouth fell open as her face registered, not
just shock, but total disbelief.

'I have this gene,' he went on whilst she just sat there,
staring at him with stunned eyes. 'All the men in our
family have it. Actually, now that I come to think of it,
there are only men in our family. Except for their wives,
of course. But they don't carry the same blood.'

She blinked. It was the first movement he'd noted
since he told her how long ago he'd rendered himself
sterile. Clearly, she was in deep shock.

Good, he thought. It would give him time to explain.

'My father didn't commit suicide because of gam-
bling losses,' he went on. 'I believe he did it because
he'd begun experiencing the first signs that his mind had
begun to deteriorate. That's what this gene causes. Early
onset dementia, or Alzheimer's, if you want the more

technical term. I found out the truth not long after my father died. My aunt Fenella told me. She was married to my dad's older brother. I knew my uncle had suffered from dementia before he died but I had no idea that it ran through the family tree the way it did. My grandfather also had it, apparently, and my great-grandfather. Aunt Fenella did some research and discovered that they all had begun to lose it around fifty years old. She said she was only telling me to stop me from having children and passing on the gene to another generation. She said it was a shame that my father hadn't realised the situation before he'd had me. Apparently, Uncle George had had his suspicions and had refused to have kids. Unfortunately, he and my dad were always at loggerheads with each other and hadn't spoken in years. She said she was sorry to have to tell me such bad news but felt it was her duty.'

Warwick dragged in some much-needed breath before continuing his harrowing tale. 'I have to confess I wasn't too happy with her at the time. I'd never suspected a thing, you see. My grandfather died when I was a very small boy so I never knew what ailed him. To me he was just an old man in a wheelchair. My grandmother never enlightened me. Maybe she didn't know back then that it could be inherited. She died when I was eight, leaving me a whole heap of money in trust because she didn't approve of my father's hedonistic lifestyle. I used to disapprove of his amoral behaviour as well, till I found out why he'd gone off the rails the way he had. Down deep, he must have suspected what might happen to him. Like they say, you shouldn't judge a man till you've walked a mile in his shoes. Well, I've walked in my father's shoes for the last twenty years and, I can tell you, it's not a very pleasant experience.'

'Oh, Warwick…'

'Please don't cry. I couldn't bear it if you cry.'

Amber struggled to fight back the tears. And she managed, on the surface. Inside, she was still weeping. But not for herself—for him. How dreadful it must have been to have found out at twenty that you had no hope of living a long happy life; that you were condemned to a future where you knew nobody and remembered nothing. Bad enough at seventy, or eighty, but at fifty? It didn't bear thinking about.

But she *had* to think about it. She had to find a way to make what life Warwick did have left be filled to the brim with happiness.

'If you didn't have this gene,' she said, 'would you have got married and had children?'

'I don't believe in what ifs, Amber. I do have this gene and nothing can change that.'

'Are you sure? I mean, are you absolutely sure? Have you been tested? They have tests for such things, don't they? I know they do.'

Warwick frowned at her questions. In actual fact he hadn't been tested. There hadn't been an accurate test twenty years ago. But he'd known the truth, as his aunt Fenella had known the truth. With some further research he'd found out that there were others in his family line who had gone the same way.

In view of this cast-iron evidence, he'd taken what actions were necessary to make sure he never passed on the flawed gene. When a test had become available in more recent years, he'd thought about having it, then dismissed the idea as a total waste of time.

'You haven't been tested, have you?' Amber swept on.

'No.'

'Good heavens, why not?'

Warwick shrugged. 'By the time a test became available, it seemed…pointless.'

'How can you say that? Genes are known to skip generations. Or become recessive. Or whatever it is genes do!'

'In my family this gene has not skipped a single generation.'

'Maybe not, but miracles do happen, Warwick. I thought you would never fall in love with me,' she said. 'But you have, haven't you?'

How could he lie? If nothing else, she deserved the memory of his loving her.

'Yes,' he said, and for the first time in twenty years he felt tears well up in his own eyes. But to start weeping was unthinkable.

'I must go,' he said, and stood up abruptly.

'But you can't go!' Amber cried, and swung her legs over the side of the bed, wincing when she tried to stand up without the walking stick.

'For goodness' sake, woman,' he ground out as he settled her back on the side of the bed, 'I'm only going out to the kitchen. The ice cream's probably melted by now.'

'I don't give a hoot about the ice cream. I'm not letting you leave this room till you promise me to go and have that test.'

He sighed. 'Amber, I—'

'If you love me at all then you'll promise me.'

'And when it comes back positive?'

'Then we'll know for sure and we'll deal with it. *We*, Warwick: you and me together. That's what love is all about. Being there for the person you love, through good times and bad.'

'But all I can offer you is bad.'

'That's not true. We could still get married and have a child. We could adopt. You're wealthy. We could get a baby from Asia without waiting too long. An orphan in need of a good home. You're only forty, Warwick. You have years and years of good life ahead of you.'

'No more than ten, Amber,' he reminded her harshly. 'And what then? You'd nurse me until I wouldn't even recognise who you are? I know you. You wouldn't put me in a nursing home. I'd be like a millstone around your neck until the day I died. Sorry, Amber, but I love you too much to put you through that. You deserve better out of life. You deserve a man who's going to be there for you and your children until they grow up, a man who can make love to you and make you happy.'

'Please don't do this, Warwick,' she sobbed. 'Please don't leave me.'

'I have to, Amber.'

'No, you don't. Not yet. Look, forget marriage and children. We could still have a lot of good years together. We could travel and make love and…and…'

'No, Amber. Trust me to do the right thing here at long last. I have to leave and let you get on with your own life.'

'No, no, no!' she cried, shaking her head violently from side to side. 'You don't understand. I won't get on with my own life. I'll never love anyone else the way I love you. I'll never get married. I'll die in this place a lonely old maid, just like Aunt Kate.'

Warwick ached to take her in his arms and say he would do whatever she wanted. But he knew he would hate himself in the end if he weakened.

'That's your choice, Amber. But you don't have to die lonely. I'm sure there are plenty of men out there who will happily give you what you want. Though, for crying out loud, don't try Jim Hansen! Find someone nice, a man who comes from a good family. Check out what kind of man his father is. That'll give you a good guide. And make sure he's healthy.'

Amber clamped her hands hard over her ears. 'I'm not listening to any more of this. You're not going to leave, you're going to stay, and we're going to work something out.'

Gently, he took her hands away from her ears and looked her straight in the eye.

'I'm sorry, Amber,' he said firmly, even though his heart was breaking, 'but I *am* going to leave. I *have* to. There's nothing you can say to change my mind, I'm afraid.' He let go of her hands and stood up. 'I'll go and put away the food first, then I'll pack my things and make my way. You should be able to manage here on your own now, if you use your common sense and be careful, and move back into this room. I'm sure Tara and Max will help. And your mother, too, if you ask her.'

'No!' she cried. 'Don't leave me, Warwick. Please don't leave me.'

'Amber,' he said, his eyes tormented, 'don't make this any harder for me than it is.'

She saw, then, that there was nothing she could say to make him stay. Saw, also, how much he loved her. So much so that he was prepared to sacrifice his own happiness for hers.

It was a humbling realisation but a strangely em-powering one. If he could do this for her, then the least she could do was accept his decision with dignity and grace.

'Promise me one thing before you go,' she said softly.

Warwick frowned. 'What?'

'You'll have that gene test.'

'Amber, I—'

'It's not too much to ask, surely.'

'Very well,' he agreed, if somewhat reluctantly.

'Give me your solemn word,' she insisted.

'You have it. Now I really must go.'

CHAPTER EIGHTEEN

'HAVE you heard from him?' Tara asked.

'No,' Amber replied.

They were sitting out on the terrace of Tara's house, having coffee. They were alone, Max having taken Stevie and Jasmine for a walk along the beach. The strong winds of the day before had abated, and the sky was blue and the sun was out.

It had been two weeks since Warwick had left. Two weeks during which Amber had done a lot of thinking and talking.

Confiding in Tara and Max had been a very wise decision. They'd stopped her from becoming too depressed or maudlin. She hadn't, however, told her mother yet that her relationship with Warwick was over. Whenever Doreen rang, Amber pretended everything was fine. That was easier than launching into the explanation of why he'd left. One day, she would explain, but not right now.

'He should have had the results of the gene test by now,' Tara pointed out.

'I would imagine so,' Amber replied with a jagged twist to her heart. 'Obviously it came back positive.'

Tara sighed. 'I know it's hard to accept, Amber,

loving the man the way you do. But perhaps it's all for the best that he's gone.'

'No, it's not,' Amber replied with a fierceness that betrayed how upset she still was. 'I could have made him happy, if he'd let me.'

'You already made him happy. You showed him what love was and taught him how to love in return.'

'Maybe. But I'm afraid, Tara. Afraid of what he's going to do when things start to go wrong and there's no one there to love him and look after him.'

'You don't think he's going to commit suicide like his father did?'

'I *know* he will.'

'Oh, Amber…'

Amber stood up abruptly. 'I have to go to him. I have to make him understand that when you love someone you can't just forget them like that. I…Oh, my God!' she gasped. 'Warwick!'

Tara's eyes whipped up to see the man himself walking across the sand towards them. Max was with him, carrying Stevie, Jasmine having bolted on ahead. She burst through the back gate and ran up onto the terrace, her pretty little face highly animated.

'Uncle Wawie's come back!' she cried. 'You were *wong*, Mummy. He hasn't gone.'

'So it seems, darling,' Tara replied.

Despite her heart having leapt up into her mouth, Amber tried not to read too much into Warwick's unexpected visit.

Maybe he'd just come to say a last goodbye before leaving Australia. Maybe he'd brought her the rest of her things from his Sydney apartment. Maybe he…

No, no. She dared not hope that that test had come back negative. That would be nothing short of a miracle.

Her eyes went to his as he came into the backyard. There was no great joy in them, she noted. He actually looked very tired. Her heart sank again, that foolish heart that couldn't seem to stop hoping for miracles.

'Hello, Amber...Tara,' he said as he stepped up onto the terrace. 'Sorry to drop in on you like this. But I needed to talk to Amber and I didn't want to do it over the phone. When you weren't at home,' he directed straight at Amber, 'I guessed you might be here.'

'She drops in most afternoons,' Tara said.

Warwick frowned at Amber. 'I sure hope you didn't get here by way of the beach. Walking across that soft sand would be much too hard on your newly healed ankle.'

Amber had to smile. He really couldn't get out of the habit of running her life for her.

'No, Warwick, I didn't walk, I drove. And before you say anything more, I am allowed to drive.'

'Tara,' Max said as he joined them. 'Warwick wants to have a private word with Amber, so what say we take these kids upstairs for a bath and leave them to it?'

'But I don't *want* a bath,' Jasmine wailed when her mother scooped her up. 'I want to stay with Uncle Wawie.'

'It's all right, sweetie,' Warwick told her. 'I'll still be here when you've finished your bath.'

'You will?' a stunned Amber said once the others had gone.

'Yes,' he said and sat down beside her.

Amber swallowed. 'I'm not sure I understand. Did your gene test come back negative? Is that why you're here?'

'No. This has nothing to do with any gene test.'

'You did have it, didn't you? You gave me your solemn word.'

'Yes, I had it done last week. But I haven't received the results yet, though they should be through any time now. They did say, however, not to get my hopes up. Not with my family history. Frankly, I only did it because you asked me to.'

'I see.' Amber was beginning to feel confused. 'So why *are* you here, then?'

'Well you might ask. I really was determined to leave you, my darling. Quite determined. Determined to leave Australia as well, never to return. I've already put the apartment up for sale. But then I had this telephone call from Max last night, and he asked me what I'd have done if I had been perfectly well and it had been *you* who'd had the bad gene. He set me thinking. Actually I stayed up all night. And I finally realised that my so-called noble sacrifice in leaving you was not so noble after all. I mistakenly thought I was saving you from unhappiness in the future,' he said. 'Instead, I was condemning you to unhappiness right now, and possibly for the rest of your life. I knew if our situations were reversed I would not want to leave you. So, if you still love me, my darling,' he said, taking her hands in his and lifting them up to his lips, 'if you still have the courage…would you do me the honour of becoming my wife?'

Amber could not stop the tears from flooding her eyes.

This time, he didn't tell her not to cry. Instead, he gathered her close and held her whilst she sobbed quietly against his chest. And it was whilst he was holding her that Warwick heard the sound of his phone ringing.

'Damn it,' he muttered. 'Sorry, darling.' He disengaged himself from her arms and reached for the handset in his back pocket. 'It's probably my estate agent with an offer. He was showing a few people around the apartment today. I really should answer it and tell him I'm not selling after all.'

It wasn't the agent. It was the professor who'd taken charge of his gene test and who'd been extremely interested in Warwick's case.

'The results have just come in,' the professor said. 'You left your phone number so I thought I should ring you straight away.'

'That was most considerate of you.' Despite knowing what he was about to say Warwick couldn't help the tightening in his chest.

'It's negative, Mr Kincaid. You do not have the early onset Alzheimer's gene.'

'*What? Are* you sure? There couldn't have been a mistake made?'

'There have been no mistakes. I double checked everything. Of course this doesn't mean you won't get dementia at some stage in your life. But the risk is no greater than for anyone else.'

'I can't believe it.' And he couldn't: his heart was pounding and his head was spinning.

'I have to admit that I was surprised after the family history you gave me. I can only think that perhaps the man you thought was your father is not really your biological father. Such things do happen, you know. In any case, it's good news, isn't it?'

'Very good news. Thank you so much for calling me.'

'My pleasure.'

The professor hung up and Warwick turned his eyes to look at Amber.

'I still can't believe it,' he said, only just managing to hold on to his emotions.

'What is it?' Amber asked. 'What's happened?'

'That was Professor Jenkins, from the laboratory where I had my gene test done. The result was negative.'

'Oh, my God! Oh, Warwick. Is he sure? They couldn't have made a mistake, could they?'

'That's the first thing I asked him. But no, he said he double checked everything and he's quite sure.'

'Oh, Warwick, oh, dear, I know I'm going to cry again.'

'That's perfectly all right, my darling,' Warwick choked out as he pulled her into his arms. 'I think I'll join you.'

By the time Max returned downstairs, all weeping had stopped and two joyous faces turned to meet his enquiring eyes.

'Clearly she said yes,' Max said to Warwick.

'Yes,' Warwick replied, smiling.

'Sounds like a good excuse to break out a bottle of my best champagne.'

'Before you do that I have some other good news,' Warwick said.

'Really? What?'

'The results of my gene test came back negative.'

'You're kidding me. Wow. This is truly great news. I'll have to go tell Tara straight away. Tara?' he called out as he raced back into the house. 'Guess what?'

'You do realise what my negative result means, Amber,' Warwick said whilst waiting for their friends to reappear.

'Not really. What do you mean?'

'The professor suggested it's highly likely that the

man I thought was my father is *not* my father. That's got me thinking. Under the circumstances, I feel I should go to London and ask my long-lost mother a few questions. I know she lives there somewhere. Would you like to come with me?'

'Just try and stop me.'

'And whilst we're in London, I'll make enquiries about who's the best man for the job of reversing my vasectomy. I know it's possible because the doctor who did my original operation thought I might change my mind at some stage so he made sure that it could be reversed.'

'In that case, why can't *that* doctor do the reversal?'

'Darling, that was twenty years ago. He's probably an old dodderer by now with shaking hands and bad eyesight. No, I'll find a younger man, an expert in the field. We don't want anything getting between you and your babies, do we?'

Till the day he died, Warwick would always remember the look on her face at that moment.

CHAPTER NINETEEN

Less than a week later, Amber and Warwick were standing on the doorstep of his mother's very smart town house in Kensington, waiting for someone to answer the doorbell. They had telephoned beforehand, having received the address and phone number from the private investigator Warwick had hired a week earlier. His mother had sounded agitated at the prospect of her long-estranged son visiting her, but had agreed in the end when he'd said it was a matter of some importance, though he hadn't elaborated further.

'How old would she be now?' Amber whispered to him as they waited, hand in hand.

'Sixty,' he replied. 'She was twenty when I was born. Twenty-one when my father divorced her.'

Amber frowned. 'Goodness. That was very young to be married and divorced.'

The woman who answered the door didn't look sixty. She didn't even look fifty: she could have easily passed for forty-five, her handsome face unlined, her figure superb, her obviously dyed red hair exquisitely groomed. But, despite her striking looks, Gloria Madison had never made it big in the acting world, her career having been relegated to minor roles in lesser movies. Nowadays, she rarely got a part at all.

For a long moment she just stared at Warwick.

'My goodness,' she said, a red-nailed hand lifting to rest at the base of her throat. 'You're the spitting image of him.'

'Of whom?' Warwick returned coldly.

Gloria blinked, her gaze shifting abruptly to Amber before returning to Warwick.

'Your father, of course,' she said somewhat brusquely.

'And who, exactly, was my father?' he shot back.

'What? What kind of strange question is that? You know very well who your father was!'

'I know who I *thought* he was.'

Heat reddened Gloria's already rouged cheeks. 'What are you suggesting? If you think I cheated on your father when we were married, then you'd be very wrong indeed. I wouldn't have dared.'

Warwick's hand tightened around Amber's. Suddenly, it worried him that somehow that test result might have been wrong. Mistakes did happen, no matter what the professor said.

'Can we come inside, Mother? I really don't want to discuss what is a highly personal situation out in the street.'

'Oh, very well. But you will have to be quick. I'm expecting a visitor in half an hour.'

A man, no doubt, Amber thought as she looked Warwick's mother up and down. You didn't wear an outfit like that for a woman friend.

Gloria led them into an elegantly furnished reception room where she waved them over to the cream sofa that sat beneath an elaborately dressed bay window. She then lowered herself stiffly into a matching armchair that faced them. Warwick introduced Amber, but Gloria didn't say anything to her.

Amber could see the woman was very nervous. Why be so, unless she was lying?

'Warwick wants to have a DNA test done,' Amber invented suddenly, despite knowing that was impossible, since there was no one on his father's side left alive to get samples from. 'That way it can be confirmed that his father really was his father.'

Alarm flashed into the woman's face. 'But, why, for heaven's sake?'

Amber leaned in to Warwick. 'I think she's lying about having cheated during her marriage,' she murmured.

Warwick was beginning to think so too. Maybe if he told her the truth…

'You probably don't know this, Mother, but there is a gene in the Kincaid family which produces early onset Alzheimer's. Dad inherited it. But I don't think he realised this fact till after I was born. It's the real reason he committed suicide. The symptoms usually start around fifty.'

'Good Lord!' Gloria gasped. 'Oh, how awful! No, I never knew. Honestly.' A frown gathered on her high forehead, her blue eyes clouding with real distress. 'But I…I think you're wrong about James not knowing this before you were born, Warwick. He must have known. It's why he did what he did. Why he—' She broke off, her feelings of being flustered filling her face.

'What did he do?' Amber jumped in immediately.

Gloria stared at her before her eyes swung suddenly to Warwick's. 'Are you saying you've believed all this time that *you've* inherited that dreadful disease?'

Warwick's heart skipped a beat as he heard the

inference behind his mother's words. 'Are you admitting that James Kincaid wasn't my biological father?'

'I…I promised to never say anything,' Gloria cried. 'I signed a legally binding contract. James paid me a lot of money to do what he wanted me to do.'

'And what was that, exactly?'

'To marry him and have you, but then to divorce him and give you up. He said he wanted a child, but not a wife.'

Warwick's confusion was acute. 'So James Kincaid *was* my biological father.'

'No, no, he wasn't!' she confessed. 'I didn't even meet James till I was four months pregnant with you.'

Amber and Warwick just stared at her.

'I'm so sorry,' Gloria blurted out, 'so terribly terribly sorry. But how was I to know? James never said a word about inheriting Alzheimer's to me.'

'I see,' Warwick bit out as shock over her revelations set in. His hands actually began to shake. 'Do you think Mother, that I might have a spot of whisky, or brandy? Whatever you have.'

'Yes, of course.' And she jumped up.

'Me too,' Amber said, her hand tightening around Warwick's.

His mother returned with two balloons of brandy—very good brandy, actually. Considering the lack of success in her acting career she must have received an extremely generous settlement for giving up her son. Strangely, this thought didn't upset Warwick. He wasn't at all bonded with the woman, or the man who'd fathered him.

Though he *was* curious.

'When you said I was the spitting image of him,' he

began after swallowing a reviving gulp of brandy, 'you meant my biological father, didn't you?'

'Yes,' she said with an almost wistful sigh. 'Though you're not unlike James. I was always attracted to the tall, dark and handsome type, usually with blue eyes. So when you were born people readily believed you were James's son.'

'Who *is* my real father, then?' Warwick asked.

'A man called Alistair Johnson. He was an actor…a married actor. I met him when I was only nineteen. He was twenty years older than me and I was crazy about him. When I fell pregnant, I thought I could get him to leave his wife and marry me. When I didn't go through with the termination he'd arranged, he still refused. Said his wife knew he slept around and didn't care.' Remembered distress flickered across her face. 'I didn't want to have a baby by myself. It was hard back then, being a single mother. I knew my family wouldn't help me. I'd run away from home when I was only fourteen to become an actress. They told me to never go back, and they meant it.'

For a long moment, Gloria looked truly sad and regretful. Amber felt a little sorry for her. As much as she had her differences with her own family, she knew they would never do something like that; they would never disown her.

Gloria sighed, then straightened her shoulders in a telling gesture. It reminded Amber of Warwick and the way he straightened his shoulders sometimes.

'I met James at a party,' Gloria continued. 'He seduced me with surprising ease, and it was during the first night we spent together that I confessed my predicament to him. You could have knocked me over with a feather when he said he would marry me and raise my baby as his own. But only if I took myself totally out of the picture. He said he wanted a legitimate child whom people recognised as his own, but not a wife.'

Amber took another sip of brandy to hide her shock. What kind of man made a proposition like that?

'He told me that he'd had cancer as a young man, and several bouts of radiation therapy had rendered him sterile,' Gloria elaborated. 'Which I totally believed. But now that I know the truth, I suspect James might have already got himself a vasectomy so that he couldn't have children. The man I married would not have risked passing on that horrible gene you told me about. James was too intelligent to let that happen.'

Warwick could only nod in agreement. It was, after all, what he had done himself.

'I know you probably both think it was terrible of me to take money to give up my baby, but back then it seemed the best solution. I was only young and silly and, yes, ambitious. If it means anything to you,' she said, looking directly at Warwick with sad eyes, 'then I have thought of you often.'

'And I you,' he returned, not at all warmly.

'Oh, dear,' she said somewhat brokenly. 'I suppose it's too late to ask for your forgiveness.'

'Much too late,' Warwick bit out.

'It's never too late for forgiveness,' Amber piped up beside him. 'This is your mother, Warwick. The grand-mother of your future children. I refuse to leave this house till you've made peace with each other.'

Both of them stared at her, Gloria with surprise and Warwick with irritation. Till he remembered that this was why he'd fallen in love with Amber. Because of her kind heart and warm, loving nature. Not to mention her stubbornness. Even when she was being stubborn, she was endearing.

His sigh carried resignation. 'If I must…'

'You must,' Amber insisted.

'All right. I forgive you…Mother.'

Strangely, when he said the words, Warwick felt better. Not that he'd ever been overly bitter about his mother abandoning him. After all, he'd never known her.

Gloria tried not to cry. She'd been trying not to cry ever since she'd opened the door and seen her son for the first time in over thirty-nine years. For most of those years, she'd deeply regretted the deal she'd made with James. The guilt had eaten away at her very soul till she was little more than an empty shell.

No wonder she'd never really made it as an actress. It must have shown up on the screen, the emptiness inside, the lack of love.

Not that she was lacking in love at this moment. It came rushing back, the fierce love that she'd felt for her baby the day he was born, but which she'd quickly buried beneath her selfishness and greed.

'Thank you,' she choked out. 'And thank *you*,' she directed at the lovely girl her son had brought with him.

The girl smiled, first at her, then up at Warwick. It was the most beautiful smile Gloria had ever seen: full of love and joy. A smile she hoped to see often in the years to come.

If fate would be that kind…

'We should go now,' Warwick said, taking Amber's arm and standing up. 'Your visitor will be arriving shortly.'

Gloria stood up, too. 'There is no visitor. I lied about that.'

Amber swiftly realised that the man Gloria had dressed for had been her son.

'Why don't we take Gloria out for lunch, Warwick?' she suggested. 'It's high time we got to know one another. After all, she is going to be my future mother-in-law.'

'You're getting married!' Gloria gushed. 'How wonderful. But you're not wearing an engagement ring?' she directed at Amber.

'She will be by tonight,' Warwick said brusquely.

'So when is the wedding to be?'

'This summer,' Warwick replied firmly. 'On a lovely little beach just north of Sydney.'

'I thought I detected an Australian accent,' Gloria said, smiling at Amber. 'I've always wanted to go to Australia.'

Amber glanced up at Warwick, who shrugged his resignation over what he had to do.

And so it was, that on a brilliantly sunny day in the first week in November on Wamberal Beach, Amber Roberts became Mrs Warwick Kincaid, the simple ceremony watched by only a small group of family and friends. Max was the best man, of course, with Tara a stunningly beautiful matron of honour. But not as beautiful as the bride, in Warwick's opinion. Amber shone that day with a radiance and joy that transcended her physical beauty. He was so proud of her.

They didn't have a traditional sit-down reception afterwards, choosing to celebrate with a more informal pool party at Max's home.

Gloria, whom Warwick had flown over for the occasion, said it was the best wedding she'd ever been to.

Still, by the time Warwick and Amber flew off on

their honeymoon—they'd chosen a secluded and exclusive island resort up in the Whitsunday passage—both of them were happy to be alone. The last few months had been a rather stressful time, what with Warwick having had his vasectomy reversed, then having to wait to see if it had worked. Amber had not yet fallen pregnant and it worried Warwick that he would not be able to give her what she wanted most in the world—and what he wanted too.

So it was a highly concerned Warwick who awaited the result of another pregnancy test, which Amber took on the last day of their three-week honeymoon. Her period was only a week late, so it was possibly too early to have a definitive result.

Still…

His heart was thudding loudly in his chest by the time she emerged from the bathroom.

'Well?' he asked, unable to read the somewhat blank expression on her face.

'It went blue,' she said. 'Very blue.'

'Which means?'

'I'm pregnant, Warwick. We're going to have a baby!'

Warwick couldn't speak, a huge lump forming in his throat. Amber hurried over to where he was standing by the bed and wrapped her arms around his waist.

'You don't have to say anything,' she murmured, and laid her head against his chest. 'I know exactly how you feel…'

EPILOGUE

Excerpt from Amber's new year diary, started late in her twenty-sixth year, well after she became Mrs Kincaid, and the mother of a girl.

I haven't had much time to write in you lately, diary. Having a baby is very…time-consuming. You know, I thought I'd be able to handle being a mother just fine. I was so organised. By the time I went into labour, we'd finished redecorating the B & B at Wamberal into the most beautiful family home, with one of the guest bedrooms upstairs being turned into the prettiest pink nursery—we knew we were having a girl. But shortly after I brought little Kate home from hospital, I found myself crying one day and unable to stop. Poor Warwick didn't know what to do. He rang Tara, who had a new baby of her own. Another boy, named Lachlan. She said what I needed was some temporary help with the baby, but not a professional nanny: someone who cared about me. She suggested my mother. I was doubtful, but Warwick rang Mum anyway and she was up here in a flash. Turns out I had a mild case of post-natal depression. Mum recognised it straight away because she apparently suffered from it very badly after having me. She told me that she'd been totally unable to care for me and that Aunt Kate had taken me right away to her place for almost three months. Fortunately, I wasn't as bad as that. Still, it explained to me why Mum didn't have the same bonding with me that she had with my brothers. But you know what? During the last month of her staying here and helping me with Katie, we've become so close. Warwick's opinion of her has gone full circle, too. He thinks she's marvellous and says so all the time. Of course, Mum goes to mush and even blushed once or twice. If I hadn't witnessed it for myself I wouldn't have believed it. She's going home tomorrow and I'm going to miss her heaps. But it will be nice to have my darling Katie to myself again. She's just so adorable. Warwick says she's a clone of me but I can see him in her eyes. And she's much longer than I was as a baby. Or so my mum says. She's going to be tall—and very smart. She's already smiling and I'm sure it's not gas! Warwick said he's not going to spoil her, but you only have to see all the toys he's already bought to know that he's going to be putty in her hands. I thought Max loved his children but when I see Warwick hold Katie there's something extra special in his eyes, something miraculous.

That's what he always calls her: his little miracle.

When I think about all that's happened, I'm sure he's absolutely right…

Harlequin *Presents*

Coming Next Month

from **Harlequin Presents® EXTRA.** Available May 10, 2011.

Coming Next Month

from **Harlequin Presents®.** Available May 31, 2011.

**Visit www.HarlequinInsideRomance.com
for more information on upcoming titles!**

REQUEST YOUR FREE BOOKS!

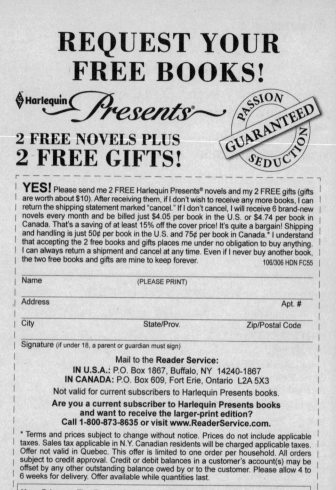

Harlequin *Presents*

PASSION GUARANTEED SEDUCTION

2 FREE NOVELS PLUS
2 FREE GIFTS!

YES! Please send me 2 FREE Harlequin Presents® novels and my 2 FREE gifts (gifts are worth about $10). After receiving them, if I don't wish to receive any more books, I can return the shipping statement marked "cancel." If I don't cancel, I will receive 6 brand-new novels every month and be billed just $4.05 per book in the U.S. or $4.74 per book in Canada. That's a saving of at least 15% off the cover price! It's quite a bargain! Shipping and handling is just 50¢ per book in the U.S. and 75¢ per book in Canada.* I understand that accepting the 2 free books and gifts places me under no obligation to buy anything. I can always return a shipment and cancel at any time. Even if I never buy another book, the two free books and gifts are mine to keep forever.

106/306 HDN FC55

Name	(PLEASE PRINT)

Address	Apt. #

City	State/Prov.	Zip/Postal Code

Signature (if under 18, a parent or guardian must sign)

Mail to the **Reader Service:**
IN U.S.A.: P.O. Box 1867, Buffalo, NY 14240-1867
IN CANADA: P.O. Box 609, Fort Erie, Ontario L2A 5X3

Not valid for current subscribers to Harlequin Presents books.

**Are you a current subscriber to Harlequin Presents books
and want to receive the larger-print edition?
Call 1-800-873-8635 or visit www.ReaderService.com.**

* Terms and prices subject to change without notice. Prices do not include applicable taxes. Sales tax applicable in N.Y. Canadian residents will be charged applicable taxes. Offer not valid in Quebec. This offer is limited to one order per household. All orders subject to credit approval. Credit or debit balances in a customer's account(s) may be offset by any other outstanding balance owed by or to the customer. Please allow 4 to 6 weeks for delivery. Offer available while quantities last.

Your Privacy—The Reader Service is committed to protecting your privacy. Our Privacy Policy is available online at www.ReaderService.com or upon request from the Reader Service.

We make a portion of our mailing list available to reputable third parties that offer products we believe may interest you. If you prefer that we not exchange your name with third parties, or if you wish to clarify or modify your communication preferences, please visit us at www.ReaderService.com/consumerschoice or write to us at Reader Service Preference Service, P.O. Box 9062, Buffalo, NY 14269. Include your complete name and address.

Harlequin® Blaze™ brings you
New York Times *and* USA TODAY *bestselling author*
Vicki Lewis Thompson with three new steamy titles
from the bestselling miniseries SONS OF CHANCE

Chance isn't just the last name of these rugged
Wyoming cowboys—it's their motto, too!

Read on for a sneak peek at the first title,
SHOULD'VE BEEN A COWBOY

Available June 2011 only from Harlequin® Blaze™.

"THANKS FOR NOT TURNING ON THE LIGHTS," Tyler said. "I'm a mess."

"Not in my book." Even in low light, Alex had a good view of her yellow shirt plastered to her body. It was all he could do not to reach for her, mud and all. But the next move needed to be hers, not his.

She slicked her wet hair back and squeezed some water out of the ends as she glanced upward. "I like the sound of the rain on a tin roof."

"Me, too."

She met his gaze briefly and looked away. "Where's the sink?"

"At the far end, beyond the last stall."

Tyler's running shoes squished as she walked down the aisle between the rows of stalls. She glanced sideways at Alex. "So how much of a cowboy are you these days? Do you ride the range and stuff?"

"I ride." He liked being able to say that. "Why?"

"Just wondered. Last summer, you were still a city boy. You even told me you weren't the cowboy type, but you're…different now."

He wasn't sure if that was a good thing or a bad thing. Maybe she preferred city boys to cowboys. "How am I different?"

"Well, you dress differently, and your hair's a little longer. Your face seems a little more chiseled, but maybe that's because of your hair. Also, there's something else, something harder to define, an attitude…"

"Are you saying I have an attitude?"

"Not in a bad way. It's more like a quiet confidence."

He was flattered, but still he had to laugh. "I just admitted a while ago that I have all kinds of doubts about this event tomorrow. That doesn't seem like quiet confidence to me."

"This isn't about your job, it's about…your…" She took a deep breath. "It's about your sex appeal, okay? I have no business talking about it, because it will only make me want to do things I shouldn't do." She started toward the end of the barn. "Now, where's that sink? We need to get cleaned up and go back to the house. Dinner is probably ready, and I—"

He spun her around and pulled her into his arms, mud and all. "Let's do those things." Then he kissed her, knowing that she would kiss him back, knowing that this time he would take that kiss where he wanted it to go. And she would let him.

Follow Tyler and Alex's wild adventures in
SHOULD'VE BEEN A COWBOY
Available June 2011 only from Harlequin® Blaze™
wherever books are sold.

Harlequin *Presents*®

brings you

USA TODAY *bestselling author*

Lucy Monroe

*with her new installment
in the much-loved miniseries*

Proud, passionate rulers—
marriage is by royal decree!

Meet Zahir and Asad—two powerful, brooding sheikhs
and masters of all they survey. They need brides,
and marriage in their kingdoms is by royal decree!

Capture a slice of royal life in this enthralling sheikh saga!

Coming in June 2011:
FOR DUTY'S SAKE

Available wherever
Harlequin Presents® books are sold.